HOLD FAST

Also by Blue Balliett

Chasing Vermeer

The Wright 3

The Calder Game

The Danger Box

Pieces and Players

BLUE BALLIETT

HOLD FAST

SCHOLASTIC INC.

For Jayden, who welcomed me to his world with a hug and an unforgettable message

This book was originally published in hardcover by Scholastic Press in 2013.

ISBN 978-0-545-29989-3

Published by Scholastic Inc. SCHOLASTIC and associated logos are trademarks and/or registered trademarks of Scholastic Inc.

12 11 10 9 8 7 6 5 4 3 15 16 17 18 19 20/0

Printed in the U.S.A. 40
This edition first printing, February 2015

The text type was set in Baskerville.
Book design by Elizabeth B. Parisi

Home, *from the Middle English* hom *and Old English* ham

> *Noun:* a place to live by choice, sometimes with family or friends; a haven; a place of origin, comfort, and often of valued memories.

By the end of the 2012 school year, an estimated thirty thousand children in the city of Chicago were without a home. This number does not include those living in the surrounding suburbs, and is thought to be low. What does thirty thousand look like? Count out thirty pennies and pretend that each one has a name. Now make one thousand groups of thirty pennies. These are our children.

Time, *from the Middle English and Old English* tima

> *Noun:* an even flow in which events occur from past through present and into future, with measurements kept by a circular system of numbers; the beat found in musical rhythms; a fated moment.

Lost, *from the Middle English* los *and the Old English* losod

> *Adjective:* missing; no longer known to be in existence; gone.

On February 16, 2003, the biggest diamond heist in history took place in Europe. Four thieves were caught, but the gems were not found.

Under pressure and over time, the mineral carbon can become diamond, the hardest and perhaps trickiest stone known to man. Although appearing to be clear, it hides every color in the rainbow. Although promising joy, it can also destroy.

CONTENTS

Ice 1
Click 3
Crash 27
Cling 65
Clutch 85
Circle 101
Crimp 127
Crack 147
Chase 167
Catch 187
Cover 205
Cast 239
Click 249
Ice 263

Ice: the third week of January 2011

It was the bitterest, meanest, darkest, coldest winter in anyone's memory, even in one of the forgotten neighborhoods of Chicago. Light and warmth seemed gone for good; mountains of gray snow and sheets of ice destroyed the geometry of sidewalk and street. Neighbors fell silent, listening beyond the *clang-scrape-chunk* of their own shovels for the snowplows that never arrived. The wind blew for so many weeks that people forgot what it felt like to walk in a straight, easy line. Life hunched over. Death whispered and whistled from around each corner. Those with homes hated to leave them, and those without wondered why they'd ever been born.

On this particular January afternoon, gusts battered the city and a temperature of zero nipped at flesh and stone alike. Suddenly: a squeal of brakes, a shout, and a thud; wheels spinning through the dusk; a blue bicycle crushed beneath a truck; a shopping bag spewing green peas, tomatoes, and oranges across snow.

At 1:11, a man was having lunch when told to notice the time. At 2:22, he was placing books on shelves and rolling a cart through math-straight channels of words. He glanced at his watch, nodded, and smiled. By 3:33, he was shrugging into his jacket, noted the line of threes, nodded again. Pulling a black sock hat over his ears, he paused inside the lobby to write for several minutes in a small notebook. "What's the rhythm, Langston?" he murmured to himself as he left the building. "What's the rhythm?"

At 4:44, the police received a 911 call from a phone booth in the South Side neighborhood of Woodlawn. A muffled voice reported an accident involving a bicyclist and an unmarked delivery truck. When a squad car arrived at the scene minutes later, the street was deserted. There were no witnesses to be found. No one could remember seeing the young man that afternoon, but there were his bike, his groceries, and his pocket notebook, which was discovered beneath a nearby car. He had vanished three blocks from home.

The truck was also gone, leaving only the slash-print of tires in snow.

Packed ice allowed no footprints. Nor was there blood.

Gone. Four miserable letters. What does the word mean? Does 4:44, a measurement made of fours but shown by three, mean a family of four is still four, even when one is gone? Can a soul hide in a three that belongs to four?

Click, *uncertain origin*

Noun: a brief, sharp sound sometimes traced to a mechanical device, as with a camera or computer; a part of some African languages.

Verb: to select; to become a success; to fit seamlessly together.

Click

Taken with a cell phone camera, this family portrait: Dashel Pearl, his wife, Summer, and their kids, Early and Jubilation, a daughter and a son. They live in Woodlawn, once feared as the home of Chicago's most powerful gang, but now a quieter place. The family sits in two tidy rows on the chipped steps of a brick building, knees to backs, parents behind kids, hands sealing the foursome. Boy by girl behind girl by boy: symmetrical and smiling. The father is pale, the mother dark, the kids cocoa and cinnamon. Eyes in this family are green, amber, and smoky topaz.

Click

Dashel takes most of the pictures, so he's rarely inside them. Here is Summer, her profile echoed by her son Jubie's, as she reads Ann Cameron's *The Stories Julian Tells* aloud to him. Here is Early on the floor, with a pillow under her head, reading Roald Dahl's *The BFG.* Chestnut hair spreads in ringlets across blue cotton. Here is a pile of books, spines turned toward the camera.

Click

Dashel Pearl offered words to his kids from the day they were born. A man who loved language almost as much as color or taste or air, he explained to his daughter, Early, that words are everywhere and for everyone.

"They're for choosing, admiring, keeping, giving. They are treasures of in*es*timable value," Early heard him say many times. Even when she didn't know what *inestimable* meant, she understood from the careful way he said it.

Dashel played a game with Early and Jubie. It began like this: He would throw his arms out and yell, "Words are free and plentiful!"

From the time they learned to talk, one or the other would shout back, "Free! Plentiful!"

Each time Dashel sat down to read aloud, book in hand, he'd look sideways and whisper, "Words are . . ."

One or both of the kids would whisper back the next three words, finishing a sentence that then opened the story. *Three words with* ee *and* if *inside them*, Early thought, *sounds that could fly: syllables that became wings with feathers and bones, weightless and yet sharp.*

Click

Here is a home in their neighborhood, one that invites dreams.

Two stories are tucked beneath a steep roof, the walls a butter yellow. White curtains frame the windows and a cat peers out. The front door is remember-me green, the echo of a pine tree; the steps leading up to it are lighter, the shade of spring leaves. On the porch, rocking chairs and an old swing wait in all weathers. Red roses bloom in the yard each summer and there's often a snowman with a carrot nose in winter. The Pearl family loves to stop and look at this house.

"One day," Dashel says, his happy boom encircling, "we'll have a home like this. A chance to stretch, to read in at least a dozen corners, and to run up and down stairs."

"A chance to cook and eat in one place, and sleep in another," Summer adds. "And to have a few secrets!"

"Like what?" Jubie squeaks, looking up at his mom. "I don't want no secrets!"

"Any," his mom says gently, her eyes dreamy. "Secrets can be lovely. They give you a chance to surprise people you love."

Jubie brightened. "Like a present!"

"Exactly."

Early was busy counting something on the front of the house. "I'd look out of each windowpane, and wait, there's twenty of them! Then I'd stick a Word of the Day on our front fence, just for people to take away in their heads."

Dashel grinned. "You my girl, Early! I'm on my way to getting us our own cozy home, and it'll feel so good, I can taste it. A home for my Sum and our babies." He put his arm around Summer and kissed her neck.

"Babies!" said Jubie, who was four. "No babies that I can see."

"You guys are embarrassing," said Early, who was eleven.

The four were silent for a moment, facing the house.

"If we had to eat beans and greens for a year — no, two years! — to get this house, would you do it, Jubie?" his sister asked.

Jubie nodded and reached for his father's hand. "Beans and greens," he repeated.

The cat in the window pressed its paw suddenly against the glass, as if to welcome them all inside.

Click

The Pearl family rents the biggest apartment they can afford. It is one room. Walk up two flights of stairs, turn right, follow a long hall with a bare bulb overhead, and you'll be at their front door, which is a dull, metallic gray. A neat sign next to the door in kid-script says *Welcome to Our Home.* Beneath the letters is a bendy bathtub shape with four circles inside — an oyster shell sheltering four pearls.

Once in the door, here's a small, cheerful world: the kitchen in one corner, across from a tiny bathroom just big enough for one; a double-bed mattress on the floor, behind a screen covered with a sunburst quilt; two neatly rolled-up sleeping bags and a pile of foam mats beneath the only window with a view. Peek out: lots of sky and an empty lot nearby, haven to tall weeds and small creatures like mice and rats. The other window is over the kitchen sink and faces a crumbling wall, one that sprouts emerald leaves and the tiniest of purple flowers.

Dozens of pillows in bright colors line the edges of the room. The floor is speckled linoleum, cream with lots of red, yellow, and blue. Lamps sit on small tables made from piles of old encyclopedias tied into neat packages with yellow police tape. A coffee table near the kitchen has low seats around it, each made from a plastic milk crate with a lawn chair cushion tied to the top. Only the bedding in the house was bought; all else was scavenged or invented.

Everything has its place. "You could eat off this floor," Dashel says, with pride. Summer adds, "And we almost do," with a grin.

Once after dinner, Jubie slithered from under the table, where he was playing trucks-in-a-tunnel, with a piece of macaroni stuck to his elbow. "Elbow macaroni," his father boomed.

Dashel reached in his pocket and, *click!*, the elbow became a story.

Click

Dashel left on his bike each workday morning, in all weathers and seasons, to reach the station and ride the train that took him to Harold Washington, the huge public library in downtown Chicago.

He worked on the sixth floor in History and Social Sciences, a tricky department that mixes fact, story, and legend. Dashel's job as Library Page, one he'd had for several years now, was to sort, shelve, deliver, and process books, and sometimes to answer the phone or update computer entries. The librarians soon realized that he was an amazing reader, a gifted and hungry thinker. They knew he wanted to earn a library science degree one day.

Dashel learned quickly that working in a library meant knowing how to find answers to almost any kind of question; it also meant understanding changes in what people want to read as well as finding a balance between the familiar and the new. A pleasure to teach, Dashel would hear or see something once and *click!* he had it.

He was obviously a Library Page who was going places.

Click

"Ono-*what*?" Early had asked the first time she heard that crazy word *onomatopoeia*.

If you discovered that a word sounded like what it meant, Dash explained, then you could add it to the family Onomatopoeia List. Sometimes Early added a little drawing as well, an invented symbol that looked like it fit the word.

She loved the *C*'s (*crash*, *click*, *catch*), the *B*'s (*blurt*, *babble*), the *I*'s (*ice*, *itch*), the *S*'s (*slip*, *slither*, *sizzle*).

Early, like Dashel, recorded stuff that made her curious, and the Pearls always had a notebook or two available. They kept a family Quote Book, for collecting wise or delicious things that other people had written, and a Word Book, where any of them could note down a word they liked and include at least part of the dictionary definition. If Jubie chose the word, someone recorded it for him.

Early learned from her dad that a dictionary is a powerful and *underestimated* kind of book. First of all, it has the shortest stories in the world, and thousands of them: stories with sounds, changing shapes, history, and mystery. Open anywhere and you'll find layers of meanings. Choices. And when you put a word in your Word Book, you can pick what you want from the definition, like picking flowers from a garden. You don't have to take everything, and that is fine.

"Gather them as you meet them. Then you'll become a part

of their story, and vice versa," Dashel said. Early wasn't sure how that worked, but she got the message: Words are alive.

Dashel explained that words can have generations of scrambled-up history — some are hundreds or even thousands of years old. They come from Old English, Middle English, Latin, Greek, Sanskrit, and many other languages — those were just a few of the roots that could be part of a word, like a root on a vegetable. Sometimes experts couldn't find a root, and then the dictionary said *origin unknown.* When the Pearls added a word to their family Word Book, Dashel called that *adopting* the word, welcoming it to a new home.

"Any word you adopt feels loved," he told his daughter, scratching his right ear, something he did when an idea was making him happy. "Language reacts, you know."

When he said this, Early pictured a word stretching and wiggling either tall or curly letters, or perhaps yawning with an O or an openmouthed C or U.

Her dad was still talking. "And when a word isn't used for a long time, it dies and just about disappears. Sometimes that's okay; it's had its day. And once in a while a new word is born."

One startling Saturday, when she'd just entered the words *adopt* and *adapt* in the Word Book, Dashel told Early that he had been adopted as a baby, like a word.

Early felt the world jiggle-slump for a moment and blurted, "What happened to your parents? Did they die?"

Dashel looked oddly blank. "I'm still wondering," he said softly. "Maybe that's why I like the family of words, the crowd of meanings. The murky origins! I've always thought about my folks but never known who they were. Always imagined a face or a voice, but never had a definition. No story.

"The Pearls, who adopted me, died in a train crash when I was three. I only remember a few details from my life with them — a crib with tall sides, an orange cat. I lived in many foster homes. Some had love and some had none."

"You're a mystery and a part of the hugest family of all, the dictionary family!" Early hurried to say, wanting to make her father feel better.

"Yes, I am." He grinned at his daughter. "I like that. So now you know why you three are so, so, so important to me. You're *critical to my existence.* And that's why we're going to own the coziest home anyone has ever had, if it's the last thing I do!"

Early reached for the Word Book to add *critical.* She liked its crunchy, delicate sounds, the crisp *C*'s and *T* together with the light *I*'s and *A*. It sounded like a crown, the fancy kind made for a king. She pictured lots of people trying it on, like Cinderella's slipper, until *click!* it landed with a perfect fit on her father's head.

Click

Early was born when her parents were still in high school. Her name came from the "promising surprise," as her parents explained it, of her arrival.

"So," Dashel liked to say, "Early Pearl equals ready, ahead, and beautiful! What more could a person want?" He added that he and Summer were the happiest people in the world when Early appeared.

Click

"What!" shouted Jubie when he overheard this. "What about special me?"

Dashel grinned and said, "Now, why do you think we called you Jubilation?" Out came *Webster's Dictionary*. Dashel then looked up the word and read the meanings aloud. It grew from a Latin verb, *jubilare*, which meant it was over a thousand years old and was used when people celebrated without worries; they were loud with joy. Jubie puffed up with pride.

"Loud! With! Joy!" he shouted.

People's names often affect who they become, Dashel explained. "Take your mother's name," he said. "The word *summer* makes thoughts of happiness and perfection pop up in most folks' minds. You know: fireflies, bugs humming in the trees, barbecue with friends on a day by the lake, lots of sun and gentle blue sky. Just like this gorgeous, promising woman here!" Summer swatted an aw-go-on at her husband, but followed it up with a grin.

"So, how about *Dashel*?" Early had asked.

"Well, that's got many facets. It's kind of flashy," Dashel said, with a wink. "The name comes from a French root, meaning a messenger. And I *do* work as one who delivers — how's that for a name fit?

"But the word *dash*, now: Are you ready? The origin is *dasshen*, Middle English. Verb, to break by striking, knocking, or hurling." He closed the dictionary on his finger and looked at the kids.

"Should I *hurl* it?" he asked.

"No!" they shrieked with delight, and Summer said, "Dash," her voice a gentle warning.

"No worries, just adding some *dash* to the moment." He grinned, reopening the volume. "Okay, now here are some of the noun meanings: a violent burst or splash; the stroke of a pen; a punctuation mark that breaks the flow of a sentence; a small but crucial addition, like a dash of salt; a sudden rush; a short, fast race; part of a famous code, the Morse code, that is all dots and dashes. Whew, what a headful *that* word is! Wish me luck." And Dashel boomed his got-it-all laugh.

This was a family of important words and their important histories. Words and life and home were all rolling together in the shell that held four.

Click

When they became parents, Dashel and Summer decided that the usual parent names didn't fit them. After trying a few things out, they settled on *Dash* and *Sum*. As they gradually became Dash + Sum + Early + Jubie, the phrase *Dashsumearlyjubie* clicked together with an irresistible *ta-ta BOOM-ta BOOM-ta* rhythm. Like a cluster of refrigerator magnets, Summer said. Hard to pull apart.

Inside every dictionary and all the special family books, Dashel wrote *Dashsumearlyjubie* in his neat, blocky letters. There were many Pearl families in the world, but only one Dashsumearlyjubie.

Click

Everyone knew the plan. Dashel would apply for a scholarship, borrow money from the bank, and get his degree. That would be when Jubie started kindergarten and Summer worked during the school day, hopefully in the neighborhood. Later on, when Dash was a full-time librarian, she'd go to a college or university, too, maybe to get a guidance counselor's degree. She liked the idea of helping teens who weren't getting much advice or support. And one day the Pearls would have their home, and everyone would head home after a long day, to a place that would be theirs forever. Early loved the slow way Dash said *head home*, as if those two words felt good to say.

The most treasured thing they owned, their family plan, was invisible, but everyone felt as if it were as solid as a building. As dependable as a road. It was there, and theirs, and that was all there was to it. It was Dashsumearlyjubie.

Click

Dashel told stories about his favorite teacher, Mr. Skip Waive, who'd been a poet teaching deep on the South Side of Chicago. He was "tough and skinny as a stick and as pale as skim milk," and used a small Fourth-of-July flag as a pointer. He'd been arrested a bunch as a teenager, but somehow got straightened out and into college. How that happened he never got around to telling them.

"No offense intended," he'd say, sticking the flag behind one ear, "but our flag is about the best tool I could imagine! Doesn't belong in a corner." When he tapped it on the board, the fabric waving caught everyone's attention. Once it snagged in his necktie. Sometimes it got covered with chalk. "A symbol packed with usable power," he'd say, giving it a shake.

There was something in Mr. Waive's teaching voice that made his students hush up and listen. Dashel said it was a beat, timing that turned whatever he said into a once-in-a-lifetime secret, a glittery gem of information that you'd be a fool to miss. Something that made his South Side kids believe that what he was sharing could shape their lives. That numbers and words mattered; they were out-in-the-open valuables that could be used in a million ways. Used and kept, no stealing necessary. No locks to pick! No cops to trick!

"I am here as a *catalyst*," he liked to say. "Look it up! I *enable*. I give, you take it away! Send me a postcard when you get there."

Mr. Waive acted like rhythm and numbers and words were all part of the same subject. Mathematics, he said, was a search for order, pattern, and beauty. Arithmetic and numbers fit inside that definition, but didn't fill it. Language was a code, like numbers, he said, and depended just as much on rhythm for its power. One of Mr. Waive's favorite poems was by Langston Hughes, and Dashel could still recite it:

Problems

2 and 2 are 4.
4 and 4 are 8.

But what would happen
If the last 4 was late?

And how would it be
If one 2 was me?

Or if the first 4 was you
Divided by 2?

"Huh?" Early had asked, the first time he recited the poem for her. "What does *that* mean?"

Her father laughed. "It's the story of most of our lives. What do *you* think it means?"

"I think it means you're confused!" she shouted, and they both laughed. "How can a person be a number?" she said.

"How can a 4 not be what it looks like?" Dashel shot back.

Click

For the last month, two boxes of books a week arrived at their apartment. Dashel explained that an international bookseller by the name of Lyman Scrub had sent them to be sold in Chicago.

Although Dash had never met him, his new friend, Al, who had been hired as a Library Page around Thanksgiving time, had. Dash described Al as a jumpy but "clever as clover" guy, someone who loved playing around with words and numbers. Al told Dash that Mr. Scrub had approached him in the stacks on the sixth floor at Harold Washington one day, saying that he needed two strong young Library Pages to help him process and transport some old books. This would be after library hours, of course. Al picked Dash, who said yes almost before the question was asked.

As Mr. Scrub had explained it to Al, wealthy book collectors often donated their personal libraries to a larger one when they died, and although many of these thousands of estate books were kept, hundreds weren't, especially if the library already owned copies. These extras could then be sold, and this was where Mr. Scrub came in.

Dash explained to Early that his part of the job was to make a list, box by box, of what arrived at the Pearl apartment, including the author's name, full title, publisher, date of publication, and number of the printing. After the list was made, Dash was told to sign it and slip it in with the books before resealing the box with packing tape.

"What's a printing?" Early had asked. She loved the way her father shared information; his tone always made a plain old fact feel like something special.

"Books are produced in batches, and the first printing is like the first batch of cookies from the oven. It's the one everyone wants," Dash replied, giving her a wink. "It's funny math, because the number of books printed also matters. If a thousand books were made in the first edition, what survives is more valuable than if ten thousand books were made. In this case, less is more."

Although Early wasn't as interested in those tiny numbers inside the front of every book, she enjoyed the way Dash shared their power with her. It was his glance at an old page, the way he tapped it gently with a finger, the way he lowered his voice that kept her listening.

Dash liked to show Early the most exotic-looking books: One had a leather cover with dragons and leafy vines pressed into it. Another was robin's-egg-blue velvet and worn bare in spots as if someone had loved it so much, they'd carried it everywhere; yet another had shiny gold on the edges of every page. Only once, he kept an old book for the Pearl family, estimating a generous value and carefully subtracting its price from what he was paid.

"An easy sell," he explained to his family with a grin.

Dash gave Al his two boxes at the end of each week, and Al gave Dash a sealed envelope with cash when he came by in his car, always in the evening, to pick up the load. Al said that he then drove the books to a secret location in Marquette Park, about ten minutes away from Woodlawn. It seemed that Mr. Scrub had his rules, and simply wanted each Library Page to do his part and keep quiet about it. Al was told not to ask what Dash was paid, and vice versa. Even Sum wasn't supposed to know.

"It's business," Dash had assured her. Early was listening; there wasn't much privacy in their small apartment.

Pleased as she was to know extra money was coming in, Sum wondered about it all. "Why would a bookseller be going through all these expensive steps instead of sending the books straight to Marquette Park himself?" she asked one evening, as Dash taped up a box with one of his tidy lists inside.

Dash shrugged. "Book people can be a bit strange." He smiled. "But who are we to judge? The world of books is big, complicated, and this guy probably likes the idea of working with employees of the Chicago Public Library. You know, as a distinction."

Sum was folding laundry and paused, frowning. "Hope it's only that," she said.

"What do you mean?" Early piped up, looking from one parent to the other.

Sum said nothing, and Dash gave her a hug. "You're as prickly as a pineapple when you get worried," he said gently. "But oh, so much sweetness underneath . . ."

Sum laughed and flapped him away with a clean T-shirt. "Okay, okay! You are one go-getter guy, Dashel Pearl. I worry sometimes that everyone in the world isn't as good as you think they are, you know?"

"Now, when have you ever heard of criminals going to a public library in order to get help selling beat-up old books?" Dash had his hands open, palms up. "Books like this aren't worth enough! I just enjoy fussing over them."

Sum laughed again. "You win," she said and reached across Early to give Dash a kiss.

Click

The book that Dash had kept was *The First Book of Rhythms*, by Langston Hughes. Written for kids, it had a red paper jacket with five wavy white lines running across it like a river. Early studied the picture of Mr. Hughes at the back and thought he looked a lot like Dash, only older and tidier. Under the jacket, the book cover was the green of new leaves.

The copy they had was worn, but a first printing, and the book was out of print; this meant there were only old copies left, no new ones for sale in stores. It was kept on a special shelf at home and no one was allowed to read it while eating.

"It's a No Sticky Fingers treasure for us to have always," Dashel explained.

Early had heard the up-down dance of Langston's language so many times in the past couple of weeks that she remembered some of the words in the book. Without looking. He'd said stuff about how each person who starts a rhythm, whether in print, a drawing, a sound, or the movement of their bodies, does it in her or his own way.

Your circles and rhythms are yours alone, Langston Hughes had written. Early had liked that. *Yours alone.* Circles. Rhythms.

Langston, Early realized when she thought about it, was an honorary Pearl. Dashsumearlyjubie had clearly adopted him.

Click

What happened at 4:44 on that grim January day was wrong. *Wrong* was the perfect sound for what the word meant: It was heavy, achingly slow, clearly impossible to erase. *Wrong.* The word had a cold, northern root as old as the Vikings.

Where was Dash? How could he have vanished into that icy, freezing moment?

No one could add up the facts; they just didn't fit. And Dash had been thinking about adding. Adding times of day to find a pattern. Or a rhythm. He'd once told Early that a pattern was something that repeated, but a rhythm had time inside it and wasn't always predictable.

Here was the last entry in her father's notebook, the one found under a car:

1:11 ~ 1 + 1 + 1 = 3
2:22 ~ 2 + 2 + 2 = 6
3:33 ~ 3 + 3 + 3 = 9
4:44 ~ 4 + 4 + 4 = 12
IF 4:44 = 12, WHAT IF 1 + 2 = 3?
IF 5:55 = 15, AND 1 + 5 = 6, DOES THAT MEAN IT'S ALL A CIRCLE? A ROLLING RHYTHM OF 3, 6, 9 WHEN YOU REPEAT ONE DIGIT IN TELLING TIME? OR JUST A BEAT OF 3s?
MUST RESEARCH NUMBER RHYTHMS.

After looking through it, the policeman had shrugged and given the notebook back to Summer. Sum had tucked it into her underwear, next to her heart, and that was where it stayed. Whenever Early asked to see it, her mother handed it over but later slipped it back in place, as if that might help to protect

Dash. Early opened the notebook now for what felt like the hundredth time in the past few days.

What on earth had Dash been thinking about when he wrote this?

He'd been trying to understand something. *A rolling rhythm of 3, 6, 9 when you repeat one digit in telling time . . . or just a beat of 3s . . .* As Early said it aloud, it made her think of Langston's poetry. Was *that* a clue?

Just thinking about her father made Early ache. *Alone! Alone! Alone!* went the painful rhythm of her heart.

"Dash!" she whispered. "Where *are* you?"

Click

Darkness. Dash's cell phone had vanished with him, taking the *click* out of all four lives. That is, if they were still four and not three.

Crash, *from the Middle English* crasschen

Verb: to break with violence; to appear uninvited.

Noun: a loud sound, the result of a person or object falling; the sudden failure of a business.

Crash, *from the Russian* krashenina

Noun: a rough fabric sometimes used to strengthen the spine of a book.

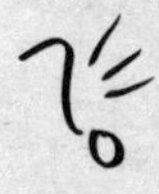

Crash

In the confusion left behind, the three Pearls found themselves in a wailing of worries, a wall of wails, a worry of walls. There were tears on top of tears, and endless fears that felt worse when shared. Summer didn't sleep. She opened the family piggy bank and counted everything inside. She called the police station many times each day, reminding them to continue looking for her husband. Early stayed home from school, not wanting to leave the other two.

The police didn't seem to take things seriously. "Lots of men disappear for a while and then turn up again," one detective told Summer.

"You're not hearing me," Summer said, her voice hard. "My husband isn't one of those men."

The detective asked questions about what Dashel did at his library job; had Summer seen anything illegal or unusual going on?

"Absolutely *not*," Summer responded. But Early knew a secret: About a week ago, she'd seen Dashel add to a thick envelope of money hidden inside one of the encyclopedias stacked under a lamp.

He had brought a load of books downstairs early one evening, after calling out, "Book business, be right back!" while Summer was reading to the kids on the bed. Early, tired of listening to Jubie's story, had moved to the other side of the screen while her mother kept reading. Wanting to finish her own book, Early opened to an exciting place.

When Dashel returned, he hadn't seen her curled up in the corner, still as a mouse. He'd stepped into the apartment, pulled an envelope from his jacket pocket, slit it open, and counted some bills. Then he'd walked quickly to the nearest stack of encyclopedias, unwrapped the yellow caution tape, and slipped a fat envelope from the middle of a volume before he realized Early was watching him.

Dash hesitated for a split second, something he rarely did, then said, "Curious? Shhhh . . . gonna surprise your Sum with this one! Not a word now, promise, or you'll get me in trouble." He slid the money into the envelope, replaced it, then retied and patted the encyclopedia table, as if to say, *Safe here!*

Early nodded, pleased to keep her father's secret. She knew Sum loved a surprise. But now Dash had disappeared. What should she do? She wished she'd never — *click!* — seen her father with that envelope.

"What should I do, Dash?" she whispered.

No answer. The promise now felt like poison.

"You'll get me in trouble," he'd said, but trouble with *whom*? Was he serious?

What if telling Sum hurt Dash? Or what if Sum felt like she had to tell the police about the money, not understanding why it should stay a secret? What if that got Dash in so much trouble that he couldn't come home?

Early was caught in a nasty circle of thoughts.

Trouble was a muddy, bad-news word, a sound that disturbed. It stuck in your mouth like gunk from the street clinging to the bottom of your shoe.

Early rarely heard a word she thought was ugly, but *trouble* was one.

Crash

Dashel Pearl had been gone for four days, and nothing was okay. Jubie whined and asked, "But when is Dash coming home?" again and again; Early felt as though someone had removed her insides, leaving her scooped-out like a melon. She felt as light and strange as she imagined the dead might feel if they could tell you about it. And Summer paced, wept, and moaned to herself and to her husband.

Early put a pillow over her ears at night so that she couldn't hear her mother murmuring, "Please, Dash, please!" over and over, her feet padding back and forth in the big room.

On day five, Early went back to school. Her friends were glad to see her, but somehow shy; her buddy Laneesha said, "Don't worry — after my dad left, it was bad for a while, but things got better. Now my mom even has a boyfriend I like, one who brought us a new TV!"

Early's face crumpled and she burst into tears. Then she sobbed, "You don't know our family! My father's not like yours! He'd never leave!" Laneesha walked away, shrugging as if to say, *You'll find out.* When one of Early's teachers stepped in with a hug and a box of tissues, Early could tell she, also, believed that Dash was gone.

When Sum asked how school had gone that day, Early said only, "Fine." She didn't want to tell her mother about the things Laneesha had said. Inside, Early decided to change the rhythm of this story, at least in public.

The next day she walked into her classroom and went up to the teacher. "My dad is home. He was doing book business, and wanted to surprise us with some good news. We might be moving to our own home." She heard herself saying it, and wondered as the words flowed out if a lie could sometimes persuade the truth to happen.

Laneesha was suspicious, and asked if she could come over to play.

"Soon," Early promised. "My mother hasn't been feeling well lately, but she'll be better." She didn't look up, not wanting to see Laneesha's expression.

Early began to spend less time with her friends at school and more with a book, especially during lunch.

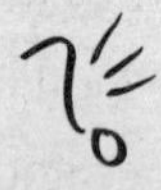

Crash

"Early, what're we gonna do, girl?" Summer moaned one night when Jubie had finished his bowl of macaroni and cheese and asked for fruit and a cookie. She'd had to tell him there was no more food for that day. He'd looked sad, but had gone off in a corner to play.

"I'm almost out of money! I shouldn't be telling you this, but we're broke, I don't have anyone to watch Jubie while I work, and I don't have a job. I guess I need to find a social service office that can maybe help us with food stamps and rent, although I'm not sure they'll do that when I'm not employed. Our bank account is close to empty. I thought we had more savings, what with Dash's book business pay, but I guess not. I tried calling my parents, but they have no phone listed now. No phone and no address. Probably just as well — I can't imagine exposing my babies to all the meanness and fighting in that household. I don't have any other family, and you know Dash doesn't. What're we gonna do?" She reached for the dish towel to wipe tears away; they'd stopped buying tissues the week before.

"Sum," Early whispered.

Her mother looked up and tilted her head. "You can talk, Jubie's busy." *"Vroom, vroom"* came from the corner.

Early blurted quickly, "I was reading one night last week when Dash came in from book business. He pulled some paper money out of his pocket and added it to an envelope hidden in one of the encyclopedia stacks. Then he saw that *I* saw and told me not to tell. He said it was a surprise for you and he didn't want me to get him in trouble. I *promised* him, but now . . ." Her voice wobbled into silence.

Her mom's face was hard to figure out. She looked partly pleased and partly shocked. "He was *hiding* it?" she asked.

Early shrugged, wiping her nose on the back of her hand. "We hide Christmas presents from each other every year, right?"

"Right," said Summer, her voice sounding stronger. "And you were right to tell me. I know you promised, but that was before . . ." She grabbed for the dish towel again and turned away, shaking her head. "This is all such a bad dream," Sum whispered. "Where *is* he?"

Early patted her mom's back, and Sum spun around and hugged her daughter tight, resting her cheek on the top of Early's head.

"Dash would want us to do this," Sum said slowly, her voice flat. She pulled scissors from the kitchen drawer and Early pointed to the volume with a swell at the edge of its pages. Sum clipped the caution tape holding the stack, pulled out the book, and flipped it open. Early watched as Sum peered cautiously into the envelope, her eyes bigger by the second.

"Dear God," she said. "What was your father up to?"

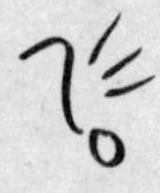

Crash

"You got money, Sum!" shouted Jubie, dropping his truck in excitement. "You! Got! Mahhhney! Let's get some cookies! Right now!"

"Shhhh," said Summer and Early at the same time. In the excitement over the envelope, neither had thought about hiding the discovery from Jubie.

Summer turned her back to the kids, and standing over the kitchen sink, counted the stack of bills. "Well, I'll be," was all she muttered. She looked out the window at the blank wall. "What on earth . . ."

Early, wanting to see, too, but realizing she had to distract Jubie, took him into bed to read aloud. "I'm reading tonight, Jubie," she said, feeling suddenly like she and her mother were in a new place together. "And I'm sure you and Sum can get some yummy cookies tomorrow."

Jubie squinted up at her. "What, you think you got big because we got money?" he asked. "Hey, Early, think Sum'll get me a new truck with that? And hey, I want Dash to take me to pick out a truck! Only Dash!" His voice cracked suddenly, and Early hurried to open the book. It was *Need a House? Call Ms. Mouse!*, a book about a mouse architect who designed unique homes for all kinds of creatures.

Soon Jubie was busy studying Lizard's house. "I like that better than Fox's house, don't you, Early? And look, I want a sunporch and a ladder just like that! And the pulley with the handle, and the net for catching bugs."

After Jubie was fast asleep, Early tiptoed into the kitchen. Sum was still standing at the counter. "Early. You gotta think hard now. We need all your good memory and brains. You know how you and Dash had time in the evenings to read and stuff while I was putting Jubie to bed? What kinds of things were you guys talking about recently?"

Early sat on the counter near her mother and crossed her arms. "Well . . . I'm thinking. He was reading a mystery writer named Agatha Christie, and also things she said about her life. Dash put some of her ideas in the Quote Book. He said her plots were very clever, that sometimes all the clues were right in front of you but perfectly hidden. Hidden in plain sight. He also said she disappeared for a while, and no one could find her. Almost as if she stepped into one of her books, then stepped out again."

"Huh," said Summer. She pulled the Quote Book off the family bookshelf and thumbed through the recent pages.

"Listen," she said. "Here are four from Agatha Christie." Sum read the following aloud, adding comments:

"The popular idea that a child forgets easily is not an accurate one. Many people go right through life in the grip of an idea which has been impressed on them in very tender years. Hmmm . . .

"The best time to plan a book is while you're doing the dishes. I love that one!

"The secret of getting ahead is getting started. Oh, yes! Don't we know it.

"Very few of us are what we seem."

Here Summer frowned, a sudden crease crumpling the hopeful expression on her face. Neither she nor Early said anything for a moment.

Sum repeated the words slowly, and the frown lifted. "Aw, he was talking about being so much smarter than the job he was doing. I know it. He had so many creative ideas, and wasn't able to use them all at work, not yet —" She stopped, quickly adding,

"He has so much brainpower, you know? He just hasn't had an opportunity to show the world yet. That's all that quote meant."

Early nodded, but both went to sleep in worried silence, a space heavy with questions and sadness. Was it really okay that she'd broken her promise to Dash? What if she and Sum were wrong? And how much money was in that envelope? She knew Sum was shocked by the amount, and wondered why . . . but no, she didn't want to hear any more of Dash's secret, no! No, no, no.

"If only Dash would walk in that door," Summer said, into the dark.

"He will, Sum," said Early, from the other side of the screen. "And meanwhile, he'd want us to use that money to eat, don't you think? He'd understand that we had to ruin his surprise."

"Of course he would, baby," said Sum. Her tone made Early's eyes fill with tears; it sounded the way their family always used to feel.

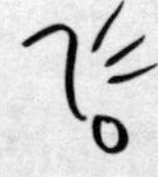

Crash

The next morning Summer pulled the envelope out from under her mattress, and while she made herself and Early tidy French braids, a 'do that always left them both feeling extra ready, she told her the plan.

"While you're in school, Jubie and I will go downtown to the library and surprise them with a visit. I've only been back once since the day Dash disappeared, and now I'd like to ask a few careful questions."

Early's stomach tightened into a worried knot. A burp of breakfast cereal came back up her throat. "You telling?" she blurted. "About, you know . . ."

"I don't want to. Not yet. Dash earned this extra for us by doing some smart work *outside of* his library job. The library may not have realized he was even doing it, and rightly so. None of their business. You know, he was so good at seeing an opportunity. He may have been on his way to earning us a home before he even got to library school!"

"But, Sum," Early said, "you don't think Dash got himself in trouble with — with — bad guys or anything, do you? Remember when you and Dash were talking about the book business and you were — well — kinda worried?"

"Early!" Summer spun her around. "Don't you allow that thought into your head, and I won't allow it into mine. Your father was way too smart and far too good for that."

"But . . . where is he?"

Summer took a deep breath then slowly blew it out. "That's why I'm going back to the library. The police don't seem to believe us when we say that Dash was not a man to run away or get himself into hot water. So Jubie and I will do a little detective work on our own."

"Don't you want me there?"

"Always! But one look at that sweet little face of yours and they'll *see* you're all ears! I want the staff and librarians to tell me anything that comes to mind, you know?"

Early nodded. "Will you remember it all and tell me later?"

"Absolutely."

Early was quiet while her mom finished the braid. She thought of her dad's note about *a beat of 3s* . . . she'd give anything for them to be a four again.

What should I do, Dash? she asked silently. Holding her breath, she waited.

The room was silent, and her head felt empty. The only sounds were her mother's breathing, the *shhhh* of the brush in her hair, and the *click-click* of Jubie's truck as it rolled over the linoleum tiles.

Crash

Lunchtime that day brought a surprise. Early had hurried off to the library room, wanting a book about Langston Hughes. Hungry for his company, she hoped that his words might somehow bring Dash closer. She found only an old, worn collection of Langston's poetry, one that hadn't been checked out for ages. She noticed inside the cover that the poet had died in 1967, almost fifty years ago. She was surprised. Dash had made him seem so alive, sharing lots of details about the man's life and some of his got-soul, gotta-sing-it poems. Now she realized something else about Langston: He liked the word *dream*.

He used it a lot. So did Dash.

She wished she had the family Quote Book to write in, but opened her school notebook instead and copied down parts of poems that caught her eye. This was something that Dash had taught her was okay: You could pick out what felt surprising in a book or a poem and then save it, as long as you also wrote down the name of the person who wrote it first.

"The quote root, kind of like the word roots in a dictionary," Early had said.

"Exactly." Dashel had beamed. "You are one girl who's putting down her *own* roots! The deeper you go, the finer you grow," he'd said, and laughed. "Hey, like my sit-up rhyme? Maybe one day someone will quote a Pearl!"

"Yeah! Sit up!" Early had said, held in the warm rhythm of her father's language.

The first poem Early kept that day in the library was one called "The Dream Keeper." It was about gathering and protecting dreams, wrapping them in "blue cloud-cloth" to keep them safe from the "too-rough fingers" of the world. She wondered if a page from one of their family notebooks, a page of dreams, could find its way to the Keeper.

Then she copied a poem called "I Dream a World," in which Langston dreamed of people of all races being able to share the riches of the earth equally, a world in which joy was like a pearl. Early swallowed hard, and kept reading.

Next she found a poem called "Dream Dust," which Early knew her father would also treasure. Langston was saying that dream dust, drawn magically from stars, earth, clouds, storms, and splinters of hail, from good and bad times, should never be for sale.

Now she was hunting, and found a long and leafy poem, "For Russell and Rowena Jelliffe" — one that seemed to twirl and fly even as it talked of roots and trunks and dreams. Early's favorite lines were:

And so the root
Becomes a trunk
And then a tree
And seeds of trees
And springtime sap
And summer shade
And autumn leaves
And shape of poems
And dreams —
And more than tree.

And so it is
With those who make
Of life a flower,
A tree, a dream.

These first four poems sang, soothing her heart, but Early crashed back to reality with the next. The title was simply "Dreams." Cold and dark, far from a joyful, sit-up message, it felt more like a warning:

Hold fast to dreams
For if dreams die
Life is a broken-winged bird
That cannot fly.

Hold fast to dreams
For when dreams go
Life is a barren field
Frozen with snow.

She looked out the library window. Snow was falling lightly, catching in feathery, winglike drifts on the sills of the brownstone opposite. Each drift seemed filled with air, the edges tapering to a whisper where they met stone. But if those were wings, Early noted, their birds were in trouble.

Wing. Root. Home. Dream. All of those Langston-y words sounded like what they meant: *wing* almost weightless, *root* digging down, and *dream* soaring. *Dreeeeeam* . . . It had a smooth, shiny sound.

Roots + Wings + Dreams = Home, Early thought suddenly to herself, sitting up straighter in her chair. Dig down, fly high, remember where you want to go, and one day you'll get there: *Roots + Wings + Dreams = Home!* That was an arithmetic sum that her Dash would approve of, she thought, with a little wriggle of pride. Having been uprooted many times as a kid, Dash didn't take a strong beginning lightly. Neither did Langston. And language, for both, was the key to survival.

The key . . .

In the next moment, clear as the snap of a carrot or the clap of a closing book, she heard Dashel's voice: *You my girl, Early. Hold fast to dreams. You can do this. Not as hard as it seems.*

Early froze, her pencil in the air. She looked around the library. A boy, working nearby, didn't seem to have heard a thing. A shocked shiver made her twist quickly and look behind herself; she peeked under the table. Nothing but her legs.

She nodded. One hand over her mouth, she whispered, "I will, Dash. I promise."

And then the thrill of hearing his voice spiraled downward into a dark pool of dread. *Did that mean* . . . She wouldn't even allow the thought into words. She pushed it away.

Push, push, *push*: Dash was fine, and had somehow sent her a message. But what did he want her to do?

She glanced at her page of Langston dream quotes, the letters now blurring through tears. With Dash, life was a step-by-step adventure, one in which the colors were sharp and the path clear. Everything felt valuable. Important. Lucky. Ripe with dreams. Worth experiencing, whether it was a poem or a neighborhood — each day mattered.

Now Early realized that a light had gone out, and the three Pearls were lost.

She was late for her next class. Leaving Langston's dreams on the table, Early ran.

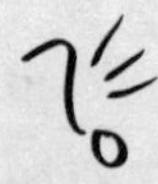

Crash

When Sum and Jubie picked her up outside school that afternoon, she knew, in a dreadful *thunk*, that something had gone wrong. Jubie handed her two animal crackers from a box he was holding under his chin, saying, "Look, Early! My own box! Sum got it for me, and there's hippos inside! And I also got a new blue truck! I'm keeping it safe in my pocket till we're home, no losing for *me*!"

It had stopped snowing but was cruelly cold outside. Jubie's coat was partly unzipped, and goo from his nose ran down his upper lip. Sum didn't seem to notice, which wasn't like her at all.

"Oh, Early!" she said. "Everything went wrong. Let's get home." They walked the next three blocks in silence, except for Jubie's pleased animal chirpings. "A tiger, *grrrrr* . . . *Ooh-ooh*, a monkey with no head! Want that one, Early?"

"Sure," she'd said quietly. *What* went wrong? She was afraid to know.

Once inside their apartment, Sum checked the lock on the door twice, and then told Jubie he could listen to a CD and also play with his new truck. She washed his hands, wiped his face, put away the box of crackers, and set him up on a pillow at the other side of the room.

She and Early stood by the kitchen sink, facing away from Jubie. Summer's hands went out, fingers spread; her eyebrows and eyes went up; her mouth went down. She squinched her eyes in two quick blinks, but the tears rolled anyway.

"Oh, Sum!" Early hugged her mother, tucking her head into Sum's neck. Summer was crying hard now, her chest heaving. She hugged her daughter back, a long squeeze, and turned away to grab the dish towel.

"Miss having tissues around here." She tried to smile. "Oh, Early. I'm so sorry, baby. I don't know what to do next. And I might've gotten us into hot water now. *Really* hot. People know about the money!" Her voice rose to a squeak. "Stupid of me! And I don't think I've even learned anything new to help us find your father. I can't think. I feel bad talking to you, but it wouldn't be right not to. It's just us three right now, and I need your help. Can't think straight, my mind is just a mess! A mess, and Dash's not here to make it okay!" The tears poured again.

"Tell me, Sum." Early tried to sound calm and grown-up, but inside she was covering her ears, screaming, *NO! No more! I'm just a kid!*

Her mother told her.

After Summer and Jubie had left that morning, they'd gone to the neighborhood bank. Dashel had opened an account a couple of years earlier.

Not wanting to use the deposit function on a cash machine, Summer waited for a teller, Jubie next to her. She had been to the bank the day after Dashel vanished, and was surprised that the account was so low — only $110. She'd withdrawn all but ten dollars, which was needed to keep the account open. Dash had handed her an everyday-expenses envelope each week at home and they'd always paid the rent in cash, so she had no idea how low their account had gotten.

That was the first shock, but she'd explained it away. And now, standing in line, Summer wondered if there was a *reason* Dash hadn't deposited that envelope of money. Why was it hidden at home?

Grabbing Jubie's hand, she'd left the bank. But on the ride down to the public library, the envelope with cash still buried deep in her purse, she turned the bank question around in her head. What had Dashel been doing? Was he planning to put cash into his book business, believing it was going to make them lots more but not wanting to worry her? And what exactly *was* that business? What kind of person was in charge? And why would her dear husband hide all that information from her? Summer had never known they had any *real* secrets — only the happy kind. And she knew that if Dashel had hidden something from her, it was only to protect Dashsumearlyjubie. But from what?

So, Sum continued telling Early, she and Jubie arrived at the big downtown library and headed up six floors to History and Social Sciences. The longtime librarian at the front desk, Mrs.

Wormser, jumped up to give them both a big hug, but she looked tired. Sum had never seen the woman so nervous and distracted, and she had eyeliner on only one eye. Bad sign.

"Any news?" the librarian asked. "I just can't believe it. He's the last, absolute *last* person in the world who'd get in any kind of trouble. I mean, *Dashel Pearl*! A man any of us would trust forever."

"Thank you," Sum replied. "Tell the police that, will you?"

Mrs. Wormser nodded, then sent them back to see the visiting supervisor, a man who had been brought in to handle budget cuts throughout the library system; he'd apparently already asked to see Summer if she came in. Sum had heard about his arrival at the library, but hadn't met him.

Mr. Wade Pincer jumped up from his chair, asked how Summer was doing, and welcomed her to his office. He found a cherry lollipop for Jubie, who sat on Sum's lap.

"Have you heard anything?" Mr. Pincer asked. He straightened his tie, which Sum said was covered with a distracting pattern of lobster claws.

Summer shook her head. "No, and I just can't understand it. I mean, Dashel! The most dependable man in all of Chicago, you know?"

The supervisor smiled and nodded. "A very intelligent and promising young man, yes. On his way. Devoted to his family, that much was obvious. It's a tragedy —" The man broke off, seeing Summer's face. "I mean, ah, it's a mystery."

"Tragedy!" Summer repeated. "You talk as if he's gone! Something has happened, but we don't know what, that's all. Speaking of mysteries" — Summer hesitated for a moment, swallowed, then went on in a rush — "did anyone here ever hear him talking about his book business?"

Mr. Pincer's face went from smooth, sweet-guy chocolate to brown steel. "What's that?" he asked.

Then he said it again. "What's that?"

"Oh, nothing, really." Summer paused again, suddenly hearing the man's suspicion. She hadn't planned to share the book business information, but now it seemed like it might be a better idea to be open; it could make things worse to hide what she knew.

Sum went on, her voice calm and steady. "My husband was learning as much as he could about old books and their value, and sometimes he had boxes arrive at our apartment and he'd go through them. Then he'd pack them up again and take them downstairs. Al, who also works at the library here, picked them up. Dash even found a special book for the family, a treasure that was unusual and that he knew we'd all love, too. He only kept it after paying for it, of course."

Here Mr. Pincer interrupted her. "Like what? What?"

Sum thought Mr. Pincer looked a little too curious at that moment, so she said, "I can't remember the name. Sorry."

The supervisor was writing on a pad. "Any library cards inside? Libraries often get rid of older books, but then you'll still see the branch name somewhere inside. Inside." Mr. Pincer was beginning to echo himself.

Summer shook her head. "Not that I remember. And by the way, is Dash's friend Al here today? I'd like to meet him and ask a few questions."

Mr. Pincer shook his head. "Not here. Not here."

"Is he sick?" Sum asked.

"Sick." Mr. Pincer nodded. "Sick. And did you ever look through the boxes with your husband? Did you?"

"Rarely. He usually opened them at a time of day when I was busy with bath time. First he'd do the dishes, then his book boxes, if he had any."

The supervisor cleared his throat. "Did these books start arriving just after his hours were reduced?"

"What?" Sum asked.

"His hours. They were cut back by twenty percent, oh, a little over a month ago. Because of the new budget restrictions."

"Oh, yes," Sum said, realizing she should work hard to hide her confusion as it didn't look good. Why hadn't Dash *told* her? Inside, she was shocked.

"Does that mean yes, they started arriving at that time?" Mr. Pincer was staring at her.

Sum looked at her hands. "About," she said, and struggled to collect herself. Darn! She would never have mentioned the book business to this creepy supervisor if she'd known the dreadful news. Poor Dash. No wonder their account was so low.

Mr. Pincer's chair squeaked abruptly, interrupting her thoughts. "Did Dashel tell you who sent him these books? Was there a name or return address on the outside of these boxes?"

"No name, just my husband's, and just our address in both the to and from parts of the label."

Mr. Pincer nodded and cleared his throat again, this time louder than before. "Did you see the person who picked up the boxes? The *person*?"

"No, but as I said, it was this guy Al, who I've actually never met. Dashel had a role to play in passing the books along, and was pleased to be doing it. He followed the directions Al gave him, making a list of what was in each box. Al paid him. The extra money went toward our savings for a home. And this was the kind of work my husband loved: rescuing old, unwanted books, giving them new life."

Summer paused here in the retelling of the story. "You okay, Early?" she asked. Her daughter nodded. "Of course I realized right away that Dash hadn't told me about his reduced hours because he didn't want any of us to worry. I'm sure he spent the extra bit of time working on his own research, the book lists and — whatever else! Reading."

They both looked over at Jubie, who was listening to a story and driving his blue truck busily up and over cushions.

Summer continued, "The supervisor then asked if I didn't think it was odd that these surplus books brought in money before they were sold. I started to get mad. I said, 'What are you implying, Mr. Pincer? You must have heard of people selling old family things to antique shops, which then sell them again. Seems to me, this is no different. The original book dealer probably liked Al and Dashel because they were Chicago Public Library employees and happy to do their part in passing along the books, being eager for anything extra. Lord knows we've made every penny we have. My husband is trustworthy and smart, learns quickly and knows how to look up things and ask questions. You *know* he is a man to trust. Plus, *the books were being picked up by someone from this library.* If anyone should be suspicious here, it should be me. I mean, where in God's name is my husband?"

Then the man looked right at her, hard, and asked, "Do you know how much money Dashel was getting for these books?"

Sum started to shake her head, and Jubie piped up, "We found MAHHHNEY inside an encyclopedia last night! A fat lump! And Sum took it to the bank but we left before I got my lollipop. And then I got a new blue truck!"

Mr. Pincer said, "Really, aren't you lucky, son!"

"And I knew we were in trouble," Sum finished.

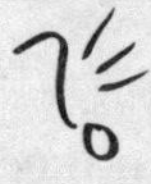

Crash

"Don't leave," Mr. Pincer had ordered, then left himself. The door banged shut.

Sum sat in stunned silence while Jubie slithered to the floor and drove his blue truck back and forth over crumbs and bits of lettuce; every few seconds he paused to flick something out of the way.

After ten long minutes, the door flew open and Mr. Pincer strode in with a police detective. Sum wondered how he'd grabbed one so quickly.

"Lyman Scrub, did you say?" the officer asked, writing busily. Summer realized then that Mr. Pincer hadn't asked her for the bookseller's name.

The detective told Mr. Pincer that they didn't have a reason to search the Pearl apartment or bother Summer any further, but that they'd try to figure out where these books were coming from and where they were going.

"Please do," Mr. Pincer said smoothly. "We're concerned."

Sum, who was getting good and angry, had asked if businesses that buy and sell used books in this country are considered criminal. Like Amazon, she'd added. Or Powell's Books.

"Of course not," the detective had said. "We just need to investigate, under the circumstances, since the sus — I mean, since the individual involved disappeared recently. After working in a building with a lot of valuable books."

"I heard that," snapped Sum. "You were going to say *suspect*! Well, what's happened to investigating the disappearance of an innocent, hardworking man? And by the way," she added to Mr. Pincer, "don't forget to help the cops figure out who-all of your current employees was coming by to pick up the books Dashel got in the mail. And count all your priceless editions, will you? All the ones Dashel may have touched! By all means!"

Sum's face was bleak, now that she was finished telling her story. "So that's it, Early," she said. "What should we do?"

"Seems like we should search this place before the police do," Early said. In every mystery she'd ever read or seen, private detectives and police had a way of getting into people's homes even when they weren't expected or invited. Sometimes that was good and sometimes bad, depending on whose side you were on.

"My thought, too." Summer was frowning. "But . . . well, what if we do find more? What then? If we start hiding things from the police and they find out, it won't look too good." Sum was quiet for a moment. "Let's have dinner. I'll read aloud right away and get Jubie to bed. Then you and I will look. It's too much to ask a four-year-old to keep a big secret like that. I mean, I can't tell him to lie to the police! That's so against everything Dash and I have taught you kids."

Early hopped up from where she'd sat down at the kitchen table. "I'll make us some franks and beans. I can do it by myself. And meanwhile, maybe you should search the mattress in case there's more money under it. Before you and Jubie go in to read."

Sum gave Early a big hug. "I'm sorry, baby, to make you help me with all these worries. I just don't know what else to do."

"It's Dashsumearlyjubie," Early said, pulling out pans and raising her voice. Then she added, "Hold fast to dreams, Sum!"

Her mother tilted her head to one side and looked at her daughter. "You are your father's girl," she said, and gave her a thank-goodness hug.

They ate. Did dishes. Summer whizzed Jubie through his bath, into his pajamas, and onto the double bed for stories. It wasn't his usual bedtime, but Jubie couldn't tell and it'd been dark for hours anyway. Plus, he'd had a big day and was yawning.

Early picked up the Quote Book and leafed through some of the entries Dash had made. She was looking for Langston poems.

First, she found the one that began, "Hold fast to dreams." With a shiver, she realized that Dash had copied this into their notebook before the gentler, happier ones. Next, another dream poem, an angrier one:

What happens to a dream deferred?

Does it dry up
like a raisin in the sun?
Or fester like a sore —
And then run?
Does it stink like rotten meat?
Or crust and sugar over —
like a syrupy sweet?

Maybe it just sags
like a heavy load.

Or does it explode?

She looked up the word *defer* and entered this in the Word Book: *Middle English root, from* deferren. *Verb: to delay; to put something off; to give in to someone else's wishes.*

That wouldn't happen to Dash's dream. "Not if it's the last thing I do," she muttered. She then turned a few more pages and found this, from a book called *The Big Sea* that Langston wrote about his life: *The only way to get a thing done is to start to do it, then keep on doing it, and finally you'll finish it. . . .*

Was there more about dreams in *The First Book of Rhythms*? A clue to Dash's thinking that might help her?

She pulled the book down from its shelf and had just settled back at the table when *BAM! BAM! BAM!* thundered through the room.

Crash

Jubie screeched in terror. Summer shrieked, "Early! Come back here!" and the girl flew behind the screen and jumped on the bed next to her mother and brother.

BAM! BAM-BAM! went the pounding on their door.

"Police!" shouted a woman's voice. "Open up, po-lice!"

"Don't move," Summer whispered, an arm around each child. "We're not letting them in. The detective said today they had no reason for a search warrant. This is too fast for them to really be the law. Not a sound now, not a sound!"

"Police!" a man's voice shouted. There were sounds of something heavy being dragged, and of hammering. "We're coming in!"

Then it was quiet. Deafeningly quiet. All three listened, their hearts pounding.

"My brave babies," Sum whispered. "They'll go away."

Jubie whimpered, "I'm scared! I want Dash!" He began to cry.

"Shhhh, we'll be fine," his mother said.

"Shouldn't we be calling 911 for help?" Early asked.

"I will," Sum said, pulling the phone out of her pocket. She began to press buttons, her hand shaking.

"Last chance!" a deep voice called through the door.

Summer said a bad word and both kids looked up at their mom. She *never* said that.

Then she stood and called out, her voice as steady and strong as she could make it, "Prove you're police! Prove it before I open my door!"

There was no response from the hall, just a scraping sound and heavy grunts. The three Pearls froze, as if not moving could make them safe. And then *ka-BASH*: a huge, earth-shattering *smash.*

The building shuddered as their front door whanged inward, landing on top of the coffee table. Wood splintered. Screaming. Shouting. Bedtime exploded into nightmare.

Early's sign outside the door, the one that said *Welcome to Our Home*, was ripped in half, the bathtub with four pearls crushed beneath a heavy boot.

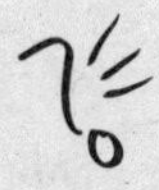

Crash

Three men and one woman, all with silver masks on their faces, black ski jackets, hats, and gloves, burst into the room. The screen hiding the double bed smacked to the floor.

"Face ta coanah ovah dea!" a man shouted, after grabbing Summer's cell phone from her hands. He stamped; plastic shattered and metal skittered across the floor. Summer grabbed the kids and pushed them down against the wall nearby, making as much of a shelter as possible with her back and open arms.

The three couldn't see what went on, but heard it — books were being thrown into boxes. Cabinet doors were ripped off their hinges. Pillows were slit open. Food was dumped on the floor.

"Don't move! Do what they say!" Summer sobbed. The kids were a painful tangle of tears and trembling knees, chins, elbows, and ankles, all packed tight against their mother's body.

The man who'd first spoken grabbed Summer by the hair and pulled her off the kids. "Wea didee keep it?" the silver face asked. *"Wea?"*

Summer, her eyes huge, said, "I don't know what you're looking for!"

The man pushed her and she fell backward, her head landing with a sickening thud on the edge of the broken coffee table. She crumpled.

"Ice!" he shouted.

She looked up, shocked and confused; he was telling her to get ice to soothe her injury? She didn't dare obey.

One hand to her head, Summer said quickly, "He kept his real book money at *work*. That's the big library downtown. Look upstairs on the sixth floor, not *here* with *us*!"

The man reached over and grabbed Early by both arms, jerking her upright. Summer spun sideways and grabbed her legs, anchoring her from below. "Yikes!" Early shrieked. The silver face was directly in front of her now, and his breath smelled like old sneakers. Old sneakers plus sweaty armpits. She saw pale skin around his eyes and nostrils, almost no lashes, and one dark mole in the middle of his lid.

"Wea egzackly? Maybe you kin come en show me! Show me afore I do somethin' to mek you *real* sad!" The man shook Early and pulled her up higher, trying to break Summer's grip.

"No!" Summer screamed. "Let go — that's all I know! Dashel Pearl would *never* put his family in danger on purpose. He didn't

tell me any details, I just know it's not here. Would you do that to your wife and kids? Hide money in your home?"

The man paused, and just as suddenly dropped Early. "I'm not kind ta liahs," he roared. "Speshly dose wid lidda ones. I'll find you tree if I need you, oh-ho, yes, I *will*! You got all ta books?"

One of the other three nodded.

That seemed to satisfy the speaker. He jerked his head across the wreckage toward their now permanently open door. The four took off, clattering at a run down the hallway, boxes in arms.

Summer sat up and hugged the kids. There were a few minutes when nothing happened but tears.

When she could speak, Sum said, "Well, we're alive. And not too hurt. Sorry I had to lie."

She dabbed her face with her sleeve and looked around. The No Sticky Fingers shelf was empty.

"Oh, Dash," she wailed. "It's all gone! Where are you? Be okay! We need you so bad!"

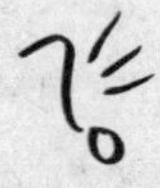

Crash

An old woman living down the hallway was the only one to appear afterward, her slippers so quiet that they didn't hear her coming. Neighbors in Woodlawn were generally afraid to open their doors at night if they heard trouble, and didn't, unless it was family or their own business. The woman, someone who had always said hello to the Pearls, had a ragged sweater on over a housedress and her hair was pulled back in a tired bun. "Oh, my," she said, shaking her head. "Oh, my."

"Can we stay with you tonight?" Summer asked. "We've never visited, but we've passed on the stairs. And I know my husband, Dash, has sometimes carried groceries for you. I'm Summer Pearl, and this is Early and Jubilation. I know it's a lot to ask, but just one night?"

The old woman was already shaking her head. "Like to say yes, but I know their kind," she said sadly. "Scum whose *business* is to frighten. They'll go after anyone to get what they want. You and the babies shouldn't be where they can find you again. No place near. You best get you to a city shelter, not even to your folks' place or the local station, which they could be watching. Criminals like that, they won't hesitate a second time. Hurry, girl. No time to waste."

The woman stepped into their home and set to work. She hustled Jubie into clean clothes and filled an ice bag for Summer's forehead, which was swelling. Sum and Early stuffed grocery bags with clothes and the only book left — oddly, it was *The First Book of Rhythms*. It had slipped beneath a newspaper under the broken coffee table.

With every step, they slid and crunched on cereal, torn

magazines, smashed dishes, slashed family photographs, unused garbage bags, supplies like screwdrivers, a broom, and a mop. Even the out-of-date encyclopedias that Dashel had turned into tables were gone. One lamp with a bulb still burning lay on its side, and Summer pulled off the crumpled shade. She held the light high so that they could get one last look. Anyone watching would have seen a woman standing like the Statue of Liberty, but without the crown, the gown, or the hope — a woman without.

"Our notebooks," Early wailed, pawing through the piles underfoot. "They took the quote and word ones! Even mine!"

"Thieves," Summer said. "They got Dash's envelope of cash and also my wallet. Every last penny! I just can't believe they took all that, on top of destroying our home."

She stamped her foot halfheartedly, then grabbed her head. "Ohhh, *ow*," she said, tears creeping into her voice. *"Yeouch."*

She turned toward the old woman. "You've been so good to us. But how do we find a shelter and get there without any money? I've never even been inside one."

"Dial 311 from a police precinct," the woman replied, her voice kind. "My, you did have you a good man, not to know that number! Shuffle along now, come quickly. Turn out that light, and turn yo' backs on the mess. My grandson down the street will drive you where you need to go."

Early could see Sum looking at the broken door. There was no way of putting it back on. The only way to fix it — to fix the whole apartment — would be to hire someone, and she knew that was impossible without money. They had to go. There was no living in an apartment without a door.

"Hurry, girl!" the old woman said. "You gotta git."

Jubie's box of animal crackers had survived, and he put his blue truck carefully inside it and closed the top. Early checked to be sure she had Langston's *Rhythms*. Summer clicked off the lamp she'd been holding, set it down gently, and gave one last look around their home; it had become a spooky landscape of destruction, a true field of broken dreams beneath the familiar streetlight that had always lit their sleep. How could that light still shine, calm and bright, when their world was gone? The wind outside had picked up, and snow peppered with ice hit the window with a *shushhh-tick-tshhhh*.

"Not did, *do*," she said softly. "I *do* have a good man. And if my husband comes looking for us, can you tell him where we've gone?"

By then the old woman was shooing them out, practically pushing them past their broken front door and down the hall to her tiny apartment. Busy dialing numbers, she didn't reply.

"They can't stay in Woodlawn," Early heard her say. "Just get them to a place where they can rest safe tonight."

Early's eyes lingered on everything familiar — the splintery stair rail, a wall stain shaped like a cat, the bulbs hanging from chains overhead — as they left the building. Sum held Jubie's hand, as well as Early's, the bags bumping between them.

A place to rest safe . . . Early had never imagined her family losing their home and fleeing into a night of unknowns, and all without Dash. The front door opened on a wall of cold.

Maybe this icy wind will help, Early thought to herself, at least by numbing the shock and pain. Ice on a wound. Ice.

Cling, *from the Old English* clingan

Verb: to hold fast; hold on; stick together; resist change.

Cling

From the backseat of the grandson's car, the three Pearls watched their neighborhood swirl away. A blanket of snow was now falling and the night was the darkest night they'd ever seen. Black was black, and white, white; there wasn't much in between until they reached the welcoming traffic of Lake Shore Drive.

Peering out the window, Early thought about how lucky the other people in their cars must be: people who knew where their fathers were, people with homes to go to, people who talked and laughed as they drove, people who weren't scared for their lives. Jubie was chewing a cracker when he suddenly wriggled and began to cry.

"We're leaving Dash behind!" he wailed. "He'll be lost!"

Summer hugged her kids, one on each side, and took a moment to reply. "Dash will find us. You *know* he will. And tonight we're going to someplace warm, where we can sleep. And you two are the bravest kids in the world. Make your Dash proud now, by being strong."

After Summer had stopped speaking, a tear rolled down one cheek. Then another, landing on Early's hand when Sum leaned forward to peer out the window.

"We're together, Sum," Early reminded her mother. Comforting her mom felt oddly easier than soothing herself, and it felt needed. "Dash would tell us to *hold fast*."

Summer nodded her head and closed her eyes. "Hold fast," she repeated slowly, as if saying a prayer. "To dreams. Dreams."

They drove the rest of the way in silence.

Cling

"Good Lord," Sum said, her arms tightening around the children.

The grandson had pulled up in front of a huge police station on the North Side. Right in front of them, officers opened the back of a van on a group of angry men and women. Soon half-dressed people in handcuffs were being dragged across the snow. A woman screamed. One of the officers punched a man who tried to kick him.

"Don't want to go there!" Jubie wailed.

Sum leaned forward to speak with her neighbor's grandson. "You've been so kind, but . . . is there another police station you'd be willing to take us to? This looks like a bad situation, and I hate to bring the children inside here."

The grandson nodded. "I don't blame you. There's a big family shelter nearby. You might not have to go through the police at all, not on a night like this."

"Your grandma told me that we had to call for help from a police station, though," Sum said, her voice thick with worry.

The grandson shrugged. "Maybe not. Let's give it a try."

Minutes later, Summer stepped out of the car in front of the entrance to an old three-story building on the North Side of the city. On the block before, they'd passed a figure wrapped head to toe in blankets and a sleeping bag, sitting motionless inside a doorway; another plodded forward in a giant coat that dragged behind, pushing a baby stroller heaped high with garbage bags. She hoped the kids hadn't seen. The temperature was a kind twenty-two degrees, kind in comparison to the many subzero nights they'd had in past weeks, but the storm was now gusting. Gusting and gnawing.

"Well, thanks so much for your generous help," Summer said to the young driver, once the three Pearls were standing on the curb, hats and gloves on and jackets zipped to the chin.

"Glad to be of help. Good luck," he said, and drove away quickly, as if eager not to linger in the area. Looking around, Summer couldn't blame him. This was one spooky place, all shadows and peeling paint.

"Well, come on, kids. Let's get out of the cold," Sum said. She and Early picked up the bags, grabbed Jubie on either side, and stepped into the entrance. Summer pulled on the door. It was locked. Then she knocked. And knocked again. There was a light inside and someone sat at a small desk.

That someone, a young man, mouthed, "Not open," and shook his head. "Curfew at eight," he mouthed. It was 8:08.

Summer threw her arms up. "Got kids! No money!" she shouted.

The young man shook his head again.

"Cold out here! Let us in!"

No response. Now Jubie was pounding on the door. Summer picked him up so the young man could see. "We need shelter!" Sum shouted.

The young man held up one finger and then waved a phone receiver. He gave Summer an open palm. "I sure hope that means five minutes!" she said. "Meanwhile, we're going to stay right here, where he can see us freezing and feel bad! Dang, we should never have gotten out of that car."

The three huddled together. "Let's sing something and jump around," Early said. "Like row, row, row your boat, gently down the stream, merrily, merrily, merrily, merrily, life is but a dream!"

"Good idea." Sum's voice was half moan. "But I can't do it with my sore head and we're definitely not merry. How about you kids pretend to be jumping rope and I'll turn?"

Early nodded, chanting, "One, two, buckle my shoe! Three, four, shut the door! Five, six, pick up sticks! Seven, eight, lay them straight! —"

Sum spun an imaginary rope while the two kids jumped up and down, their heads bobbing in front of the shelter door. Soon a car pulled around the corner — a police car. The three stopped.

As the policeman walked toward them, taking his time, Early heard Dashel's voice in her head, clear as clear could be: *You my girl, Early. You my girl.*

But what should we do? Where are you? she asked back silently, trying to send the message as hard as she could.

There was no reply. The officer said loudly, "This city shelter locks for the night at eight o'clock, ma'am. You can stay in the precinct waiting room, or I can take you to Union Station. That's open and there's vending machines."

Summer didn't move. If the policeman was surprised to see her bruised forehead, he didn't show it. "We don't have any money," Sum said. "My husband has disappeared and we were robbed tonight and our home, wrecked. I understand I have to call DSFF —"

"Yes, ma'am, DFSS," the policeman said in a matter-of-fact tone, as if Summer were making small talk about the weather. "The Department of Family and Support Services. I'll take you to the closest precinct, and they'll get you three connected to a shelter by morning."

In the back of the patrol car, looking out through wire mesh, Jubie said, "Does this mean we're criminals now?"

"Of course not, baby," Summer said. "It just means we're in hard times, but we'll be getting some help."

"And Dash will find us," Jubie added.

"Dash will find us," Summer repeated.

"Or we'll find *him*," Early said. Summer squeezed her hand.

Cling

The police station was as blindingly bright as the night outside was dark. The policeman took them over to a long wooden bench and said, "This is it. Tuck your bags under your feet.

For the washroom, ask at the desk and someone will take you. Over on the side, that's the phone, and here's the DFSS number. They'll send a van to pick you up as soon as possible."

"But, sir, I have something to report," Summer began.

"In the morning," the policeman said, walking back to his desk.

"Doesn't crime matter at night?" Sum asked, her voice getting stronger. Early was glad; it seemed like talking back was sometimes helpful.

The cop glanced at Summer as if she were a badly behaved child and then ignored her, focusing instead on paperwork. She continued speaking, her voice loud and clear, telling the officer what had occurred over the last ten days. She ended by saying, "Something terrible has happened to keep my husband away, we're terrified, have had to leave our home, have been robbed, lost our savings, and our family has done nothing wrong. Now, aren't the police supposed to protect people like us?"

Early noticed that Sum hadn't specifically mentioned finding and then losing the strange envelope with the money in it.

The cop looked up. "Ma'am, we're only staffed for emergencies at night. You can speak with another officer in the morning. Better make that call now."

Before Summer could say another thing, the doors to the precinct burst open, and a man came staggering inside, using language so ugly that Summer covered Jubie's ears with her hands and told Early to do the same. Early could hear anyway. The man was spitting at everyone close by and then vomited, right on the policeman's shoe. He was shoved roughly against a wall, and they heard the *thunk* of his head on wood paneling.

Right after, the doors burst open again and a group of teenagers came in, all handcuffed, off balance, and loud. "Drunk," Summer whispered to Early. One had cuts and scrapes all over. Another had blood and drool coming out of the side of his mouth.

No one official seemed to be too concerned. It was almost, Early thought, as if you weren't 100 percent human when you came into the police station on the wrong side of the front desk. If you were upset, it was unreasonable. If you had a question, it could wait. Just the fact that you were *there* seemed like a strike against you. Right then Early made herself a promise: She wouldn't be helpless, not ever, not if she could see a way out. She wouldn't allow that to happen. She could see that being helpless in a situation like this was dangerously close to becoming just plain *less*.

Some of the police were polite but no one was sympathetic. She knew the officers were saving lives, doing hard and scary work, and sometimes even dying themselves. She knew people who broke the law deserved to be locked up. But she still felt it was true: Being helpless could lead to even less help. She thought about Alice falling down the rabbit hole in *Alice in Wonderland*. She'd asked for help over and over, but none of the replies got her back to where she'd started.

As soon as the station quieted down, Sum made her call. She was on the phone for a while. By the time she returned to the bench, Jubie was fast asleep, his head on Early's lap.

Sum sat down. "Now we wait. They'll take us to a twenty-four-hour emergency shelter when they can locate one with space and when the DFSS van is free to pick us up. From there —" Sum stopped talking and swallowed. Early looked at her. Sum swallowed again, and wiped angrily at her cheek. "From there, who knows," she said.

Early nodded. Sum reached out and held her hand.

Cling

Dawn brought a cup of milk for the kids, coffee for Summer, and time with a kind policewoman. The three Pearls were tired, but glad to be off the wooden bench and sitting in chairs.

They were told that the police would go to the apartment to investigate. The officer asked if they'd be returning to Woodlawn, and when Sum said she didn't see how they could, the officer nodded.

"So you're waiting for the van," she said. "The city shelters are overflowing. You'll be lucky to find any sort of temporary housing at all." Sum, the officer promised, would get "further guidance" once they were in a "facility."

"But," Sum asked, "couldn't you help me with putting some pressure on the public library folks to see what's happened to my husband?"

"What's your cell phone number?" the policewoman asked.

Summer's face fell. "My phone was destroyed by one of the men last night. The same ones who wrecked our apartment and stole my wallet. Could you reach me at the shelter? Or is there any police emergency fund I could have so that I can get a phone and get to work on all this? I'll pay you back — I promise I'm good for it!"

The policewoman looked as though Summer had asked for a manicure. "I'm afraid there's no such fund," she said, pursing her lips. "They'll help you apply for TANF assistance once you're at a shelter, ma'am." When Sum looked puzzled, she added, "Temporary Assistance for Needy Families. You'll qualify with two young children." She stood, making it clear that all aid had been given.

Sum nodded, her lower lip trembling. "My husband will be back soon," she said.

"I'm sure," the officer said. "Call when you get settled, and give us a number. Perhaps someone at the station here can keep you informed."

When the van finally arrived, the driver stepped inside and barked, "Pearl? Anyone here by the name of Pearl?"

Silent with exhaustion, Sum, Early, and Jubie groped for their bags and left. As luck would have it, they were on their way back to Helping Hand, where they'd been the night before. The three looked out at a graceless, gray morning. Fresh snow had drifted across parked cars and sidewalks, but nothing twinkled. As the van pulled up outside the entrance and the Pearls climbed out, a group of smokers parted to let them through.

"Morning, dear! Hi, kids," one older man said, smiling

broadly. He was missing teeth and had a winter jacket mended with duct tape. "Things aren't so bad, now! Think there's pancakes this morning — get yourself a plateful." He reached for the door and pulled it open. Early noticed his knuckles were covered with scars and fresh scabs.

"Thank you," Summer said. "You're very kind." She gave him a half smile. "We've had a bad night."

The man threw back his head and laughed. He glanced around, and several others smiled, too. "Hold it at one, beautiful, and you'll conquer the world!" he said.

As the door closed behind them, Early heard him saying, "Sad when you first see 'em. They don't know . . ."

If Summer heard, she didn't let on.

They were inside a large room that looked like an old garage. A line of families waited for a turn at a kitchen window, where each was given a heaping plate and a glass of juice. At least fifty people sat on benches, eating over long plastic-covered tables. There were one or two fathers with young kids; the rest of the adults were women. Lots carried babies on one hip, with toddlers holding on to a sleeve or leg. One woman had two kids tied with leashes to her belt, a baby in pajamas under her arm.

"I'm hungry," Jubie said. "Can we eat?"

"Just a moment, son," Sum said. She filled out a form at the front desk, and was told that the director would be speaking with her after breakfast. She was handed three meal vouchers.

They carried their bags over to a table and put them down. "Let's get in line," Sum said. A woman sitting several feet away said, "Never walk away from anything around here unless you got eyes in the back of your head."

Sum went to pick up their stuff, and the woman murmured, "Aw, go on, I'll watch it for you. Name's Velma."

"Thanks so much." Sum tried to smile.

As the Pearls waited, someone in front of them scolded her young son. "You stand nice now, or I'll smack you! Hard, hear? I've about had it!"

The boy froze, looking up at his mother every few seconds.

Jubie stood very quietly behind him.

Breakfast was served on a heavy paper plate, with a plastic fork and spoon. It was pancakes, an orange, a slice of ham, and a small box of raisins. The kids ate.

Sum picked at her food. Velma looked over at her. "You'll get used to it," she said. "Better eat, no lunch for hours. No snacks. Where you from?"

"Woodlawn," Sum said.

"Oh, I been in that facility there," the woman said, rolling her eyes. "I was in there for ages. Getting clean. Bad times, lost my kids, but I'm doing much better. Now I'm gettin' some classes, gonna get me a job that pays. Get my babies back."

"That's great," Sum mumbled, but her face said something else. Early hoped Sum wouldn't say any more. They didn't fit here, but for purposes of survival it might be better not to show it. Every kid who went into a new grade with an unfamiliar teacher and class at the start of the school year knew this. Sum had been taken care of by Dash for so long now that she might have forgotten.

Early poked her mom. "Be friendly," she whispered.

Sum gave her a squeeze, then turned and said, "I'm Summer, and these here are my kids, Early and Jubilation."

"Them's nice names." Velma nodded.

"Wo-men!" a guard at one side of the room called out, and a long line of single women, mostly older, formed a line behind the families, vouchers in hand. Velma stood and walked slowly toward the group, then paused to call back over her shoulder, "Hold my seat and I'll be back."

Sum gave her a wave. "Will do."

The group moved forward with hardly a word spoken, many of the faces looking deeply lonely. Early couldn't help thinking of how much chatting happened in other lines, like those at a grocery store or bus stop. The guard now called out, "And the *men*!" A ripple of shuffling feet and low voices gathered in a line that snaked almost out of sight.

When Velma returned with her plate, Sum gave her a smile, then asked, "What's the best way to get help around here? Like money for a cell phone?"

The woman raised her fork in a circle and waved. "Keep askin'," she said. "You can see how many are in tough times, but just keep askin'. And stay sweet — a little sugar takes you further than gas, if you got my meanin'!" She laughed with her mouth closed, a kind rumble from deep inside. "You don't have to be drivin' the car to get where you want to go. TANF can be real helpful with bus and train tickets, maybe a phone once you get a job or signed up for classes, things like that."

“Be a squeaky wheel but talk nice.” Sum nodded. “Smart.”

“You got it, honey!” Velma leaned close and gave her a warm smile. She was missing both front teeth. “Need any advice, just ask. I’m usually in here most mealtimes.”

When Velma stood to leave, Early noticed that the woman had a bad limp and men’s army boots on. She also had a too-small pink scarf around her neck, the kind usually worn by a little girl.

Cling

The director at Helping Hand, Mrs. Happadee, had bouncy gray hair and colorful butterfly earrings but no other jewelry. Deep lines crisscrossed her forehead.

“Okay if your kids come into the office with us?” she asked.

“Absolutely,” Sum said. “Excuse our messy hair, we don’t have a brush with us. Left in kind of a hurry last night.”

Mrs. Happadee waved one plump hand. “Please. Not a problem, and I’ll give you a hygiene kit in a moment and you all can get cleaned up.”

Sum told her the story, beginning with Dash’s disappearance. The director took notes.

“So in terms of what you need immediately, it’s access to a phone so you can set up appointments, and some transportation passes so you can get around. The shelter phone may be your best bet for a while. I'm afraid there's a long list for cell phone contracts."

"Okay," Sum said. "So, we do have a home — that is, until the end of the month if we don't pay the landlord, but that doesn't even matter now, because it's been destroyed —" Sum stopped. There was a moment of silence. "Maybe we don't have a home anymore," she said, her voice barely audible. "The landlord will probably take the rest of this month's rent money to cover the wreckage."

"One step at a time," Mrs. Happadee said. "Once you're employed or signed up for job training, we can get you on a list that will eventually move you from the shelter into subsidized housing. I can connect you with childcare options, but meanwhile you three will be fed and out of the weather.

"Now. Your daughter. While you're figuring out what choices you have, we can bus her back to Woodlawn to her school, or she can attend around the corner. There's a very nice school that a lot of our kids here choose to go to. All school expenses like field trips and meals will be covered as long as you're in one of the city shelters."

Sum looked at Early. "I don't want you to have to leave your friends, but I'm not sure we want to be worrying about a long bus ride. What do you think?"

Early thought the closer she stayed to Sum and Jubie, the better.

"I'll go to the school here. For now," Early said.

Mrs. Happadee nodded approvingly, and Sum told her, "Thanks for getting Early set up."

"Do I have to go right away?" Early asked.

Mrs. Happadee said, "Better to stay busy, dear. You don't want to get behind! I'll make some calls and see if we can get you in this week. Meanwhile, shelter meals are on a strict schedule. Families with children are first in line, followed by those from the women's and then men's shelter across the street. There's a weekly sign-up for cleaning the bathrooms on your floor. Lights out and no talking or noise of any kind in the dormitory area after nine. Fighting, argumentative behavior, or substance abuse will land you out the door in a split second."

"No worries about that," Sum said faintly. Early imagined that her mother was picturing each of these things happening, just as Early was. Mrs. Happadee was trying to be helpful, but what she was saying was also scary.

"Here's what to expect, in case you're with us for a bit. If you and your kids are well behaved, we'll put you on the list for a private room to sleep in — that is, if you need to stay the full twelve weeks we offer, or even a little longer. Meanwhile, there are a lot of families to make friends with here, and I'm always around. Any guard can page me. If one of you gets sick, we'll connect you with medical care. Chicago HOPES, a wonderful after-school tutoring organization, keeps a room here with books and games in it, a place to get homework help and some one-on-one attention. All your kids have to do is show up. No planning involved. Also, you'll be meeting with counselors on a biweekly basis. They'll help you make a plan that'll get you back on the road to independent living."

Half an hour later, they were taken to a bed-and-dresser cluster in a low, open room the size of a basketball court on the second floor. The floor was chipped, worn linoleum, gray with streaks of red. Cloud-shaped stains, brown instead of white, drifted across the ceiling overhead, the shapes broken here and there by a bar of neon light. Supplies included sheets for the two sets of bunk beds, three brown blankets sealed in plastic, two white towels, two rolls of toilet paper, and three plastic kits with a toothbrush, toothpaste, mouthwash, a small brush, a comb, and a bottle of liquid clothes detergent inside. The windows in the room were small and covered with broken blinds that hung at jagged angles. A female guard sat on a chair in the corner.

"So this is your cluster," Mrs. Happadee said. "Make yourselves comfortable."

"Oh, my," Sum said. "Thank you. Wish we had our things from home so that you wouldn't have to lend us all this. Where do we store our stuff?"

"Here," Mrs. Happadee said. "In the dresser. Carry any jewelry or money on your person. Breakfast starts for families at six thirty, lunch at eleven thirty, dinner at four thirty. Each meal lasts for one hour, second servings on holidays only. You can hang your towels over the ends of the beds to dry. There's a washer and dryer on the first floor. Know where your kids are at all times, and never leave the shelter without them. Boys older than ten aren't allowed inside this open sleeping area. Boys twelve and up aren't allowed to stay in the family area of the shelter at all. You can use the shelter phone to make fifteen minutes of calls anytime between nine A.M. and four P.M., but sometimes there are lines. Local calls only. It's just up the stairs on the third floor, and patience and politeness go a long way. Everyone's call is important."

Exhausted after their night in the police station, Jubie lay down on one of the bare mattresses and immediately fell asleep. Seeing that her mother was near tears, Early patted her on the back, although she felt like crying, too. This big, spooky, open room with a lot of strangers! A new school!

"I feel sad, too, Sum," she said. Her mother sat right up.

"Of course you do," she said. "I'm so sorry. Let's get ourselves settled in here. We'll wake Jubie in an hour or so, and meanwhile we can freshen up. You go first."

Walking across the room to the bathroom, Early saw that some families had tied sheets around the sides of their bunk beds for privacy; others had hung comforters or a shower curtain. The sleeping clusters looked like a bunch of kids' forts, something you'd do for fun if you had a bunk bed at home. The buzz of radios came from inside a few of the clusters; an occasional leg or arm was visible, hanging off a bed or holding a magazine. Early saw an ankle with a rose tattoo and the message *Live for Love* on it. A baby lay on a bunk, swatting at toys hung from the wire mesh above. A tiny girl with her hair ponytailed up in a pink, frilly ribbon sat in a walker, rolling herself as far as a clothesline tied to the bunk would allow. She stopped to watch Early go by, popping one finger in her mouth when Early smiled at her. A boy Jubie's age peeked out of a bed near the bathroom and pointed a wire coat hanger at her. "Pow! Pow! Gotcha!" he said.

She pointed her plastic hygiene kit back at him. "Bang!" she said. Delighted, he fell off the bed and rolled beneath it. Early then heard him being dragged out from under by an impatient voice and told to "sit nice and behave." She then heard a slap followed by whimpering. She felt bad, having gotten him in trouble.

She'd have to warn Jubie; it didn't seem like play was allowed by some parents.

Inside the bathroom, a woman muttered to herself as she washed her hands over and over. "Not *fair*," she was saying. "He didn't *listen*. Just turned and left. Left me all alone. I *had* to, just *had* to do it, no choice. Not *fair*."

Early hadn't realized she was staring until the woman looked up and said directly to her, "Never believe 'em. Those wolves start with the nestin' and then when you got ever'thin' nice, they just go wanderin'. Always do in the end."

"Yes, ma'am," Early said, and hurried into the shower. She kept trying to shut the curtain firmly, but it drifted open. She saw the woman looking at her, just one eye reflected in the mirror over the row of sinks.

"Always do," she said again. As Early left the bathroom, the woman was still washing her hands over a full sink, the water puddling around her sneakers.

Clutch, *from the Middle English* clucchen

Verb: to hold tightly; to grasp, sometimes suddenly.

Noun: a nest of eggs; a brood of chicks.

Clutch

The paper cover was now torn, but its cheerful, familiar red was comforting, like a hug from an old friend. Amazingly, the green cloth binding beneath had made it through the attack in one piece, the spine now lumpy in places, but still strong.

Early stayed downstairs in their cluster while Sum went upstairs to call; there was no point in waking an exhausted Jubie and making him wait in line. She sat on the edge of her bunk, holding the book.

She'd heard Dash read *The First Book of Rhythms* many times, and loved the smooth, rolling sound of the poet's language. Sometimes she'd heard her father say softly, "What's the rhythm, Langston?" while thinking over a problem or making a decision. She could picture him now, mop in hand, muttering that same question while washing the floor after dinner. He didn't have a parent or grandparent to give him advice, but Langston seemed to do just as well.

Now Langston felt even more like a part of her family. Dash had told Early that this famous poet was a rainbow mix, too, like Sum and probably Dash himself: Langston had African American, white, Jewish, and Native American roots. And, like Dash, Langston had grown up without much love or a steady home. She patted the cover.

Langston, she remembered Dash saying with delight, had written *The First Book of Rhythms* after spending three months in Chicago working on poetry with kids at Lab, as everyone called it, a big and old school in the nearby neighborhood of Hyde Park. It was just blocks from their apartment. Maybe Langston had taken a walk into Woodlawn one day. Maybe he'd strolled right by their front door, long before Dash was born, and even past the house they later loved, the one with the cat in the window. Maybe he'd thought about dreams and rhythms while he walked.

Early closed her eyes and whispered, "What's the rhythm, Langston?"

Opening to a random page, she read:

Listen to your heart. . . . When you run or when you are frightened, excited, or crying, your heart beats faster. Movement of the body, or the flow of thoughts and emotions through the mind, can change the rhythm of the heart for a while. Bad thoughts upset the heart. Happy thoughts do not disturb it unless they are sudden surprises. Usually, however, the heart pumps the same number of beats a minute, steadily, once a person becomes an adult, until he leaves our world. The rhythm of the heart is the first and most important rhythm of human life.

The first and most important rhythm. Early loved the way Langston made it clear in this book that most of what people think is beautiful begins with rhythms that come from nature, rhythms that are free and plentiful. Rhythms appear in the ways flowers grow, water flows, the earth moves around the sun, the moon moves through their dreams, and thoughts travel within their minds.

She watched a vein beating in Jubie's neck. She pressed her own wrist with a thumb and caught her heart saying, *yes, yes, yes; try, try, try.* Sum was upstairs, trying to fix broken rhythms. And where was Dash? Where was his heart beating at that very moment, and what was it saying?

Turning her head away, she closed and then reopened the book. She now read:

One rhythm may start another. The rhythm of the wind in the sky will change the movements of a kite floating in the air. The rhythm of water in the sea will make a boat rock faster or slower as the water moves. Rhythm begins in movement.

If she thought of the shelter as a place filled with rhythms, it made it somehow cozier. *Rhythm begins in movement.* She needed another notebook to write in, a place to keep short ideas.

Suddenly, from across the room, there was a scream. "My baby's not breathing! He's not breathing!" A young woman's frantic voice ricocheted off the hard surfaces in the room.

Early popped up and looked around. People were running for help; the guard's chair was empty. A woman raced from the bathroom, half naked. "Who said that? Who's got my baby?" The room melted into a blur of shrieks, shouted questions, and feet *slap-slapp*ing across the linoleum.

Still no Sum, and Jubie had startled awake and was beginning to cry. Early sat back down and held him, her own thudding heart beating fast against her brother's, feeling lucky that they could cling to each other, lucky that she had him to hold and didn't have to see the young mother who rushed by, clutching a tiny bundle of blankets, her wails trailing behind as she flew down the stairs, rushing to save a rhythm not missed until it's gone.

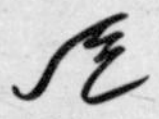

Clutch

The ambulance was downstairs for a long time, its lights whirling crazy pinwheels across the dormitory blinds. The young mother didn't return, which everyone took to be a hopeful sign.

Lunch that day was subdued. Voices were kinder. Children stayed close to their mothers, who cuddled them more. Life in the shelter, Early was learning, was a strange combination of hurry-hurry, as in getting in and out of the group bathroom fast, and wait-wait, as in waiting for food, for the phone, for meetings with people who talked with Sum about jobs, training, and where to live.

Sum was gone for what felt like hours, waiting first to call the landlord, then the bank, then the police department. As she had no personal return number for calls and fewer than fifteen minutes to stay on hold, she got nowhere that day. Her biggest worry was that Dashel would return and find their home both empty and destroyed. She wanted to leave their current address with the landlord, but he wasn't answering his phone and his voice mail was full.

That first night was the worst. Sum tucked Jubie and Early into the two lower bunks, hung clothing and coats around the outsides, and curled up in the bunk above Jubie. At nine o'clock, when the lights went out, the room was still noisy: Babies cried, little kids talked in loud voices, the metal beds creaked, the toilets continued to flush. Someone had a bad cough. The Pearl cluster was near the bathroom, so it had more light and traffic than those that were farther away. Early tried putting the pillow over her ears, but the bed beneath was too stinky and hard. Jubie was afraid, so Sum climbed in with him.

In the middle of the night, someone ran a wet hand across Early's bare foot, which was hanging over the edge of her bunk. She shrieked, and then heard a *patter-patter* of running feet. Sum banged her sore head when she popped upright to see what was the matter. The Pearls ended up that night in a single bed, barely sleeping until early morning.

Their cozy one-room rental in Woodlawn now seemed luxurious. Privacy! The freedom of choosing what and when to eat, of knowing that when you closed your eyes at night, you were safe from strangers! The freedom of a cell phone and a job! The peace of mind that comes from being with the people you love most in the world.

Each in their own way, the three Pearls mourned. They'd give anything to undo the mysterious moment that had stolen Dash on that icy, dark January afternoon. Anything.

Each tried to be brave for the other two, even Jubie, hiding their longing as they traipsed up and down the stairs and waited in line for their food. It was odd how quickly each Pearl learned that wishing aloud made everything worse. Survival was a matter of adapting, of learning how to hide in plain sight.

As she dressed that first morning inside one of the toilet stalls, hopping into jeans and a sweatshirt, Early remembered adding *adapt* to the family Word Book, and thinking she hadn't understood then what the definition meant. She hadn't known what it felt like to adapt, or how hard change could be.

Hold fast, Dash had said. *Hold fast to dreams.* The next part of Langston's poem was about life becoming like a broken bird or a field of snow if you let go. *You can do it,* Dash had said next. *Not as hard as it seems.*

But it is, Dash! It's about as hard as a rock! Early thought. As tough as a diamond, that hardest of all stones that looks as clear as glass but can easily hide a family of colors. Dash had told her what diamonds are like. And a pearl is fragile; it's never clear.

How can dreamers hold fast to their dreams when every part of life goes to survival? And how can a Pearl dreamer hide rainbows, like a diamond, without seeming to hide a thing?

Wait: Why was she thinking about hiding rainbows?

Suddenly, she could feel Dash's mind right next to her own. She wasn't alone! Dash hadn't deserted them. He was scratching his left ear, which he always did when puzzled; he'd help Early to *do it*, whatever *it* was.

Early was cheerful that morning on the way down to breakfast, and her energy spilled across Sum and Jubie like sunshine across a sill.

"I think we should explore the whole shelter today while Sum is making her calls, Jubie. Let's go on an adventure. Peek everywhere. And maybe we'll find some new books to read."

"Yeah!" Jubie said. "Maybe we'll find pirates! Pirates with swords!"

"I hope not," Sum said. She looked at her kids, one scratching her left ear, the other hopping with excitement.

"Hold fast, and beware of treasure," she added.

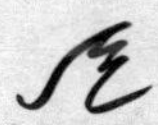

Clutch

"Don't forget, stick close if a grown-up walks by, but otherwise *spy*." Early leaned over and hissed the last word.

"Eeuuw," Jubie said, pushing her away. "You spat in my ear."

"Sorry."

"Like this?" Jubie hunched his shoulders and squinted.

Early hid a smile. "I was thinking more about detective rules. Like, see everything but pretend you haven't."

"Huh?" Jubie said, his mouth open and his tongue sticking out.

"Never mind. Just look. Then notice. The smallest detail may be the one that matters the most."

"Huh?" Jubie said. "Like me? I'm small!"

"Oh, boy," Early said. "Yeah."

"So we can find *Dash*!" Jubie crowed happily as they walked around the edge of the huge room where everyone ate their meals.

"Shhhh . . . finders need to be almost invisible. Like a lion stalking its prey," Early whispered.

Jubie stopped dead. "A lion! I'm *sad*, I finished my animal crackers! And they don't *have* 'em here!"

Early pulled Jubie into a corner. "Now look. You want to be a spy or not? Spies don't mind if they run out of treats. Their treat is finding a clue!"

Jubie looked at his sister. "Right," he said, although his lower lip trembled.

Together they circled many cardboard boxes filled with frankfurter buns, baked beans, and ketchup. Next they came to plastic grocery bags filled with clothing, stacked high in a corner. They hurried by garbage cans that needed to be cleaned and peeked inside the swing door to the kitchen. A large man in a white cooking uniform wiggled his little finger inside his ear, pulled it out for a look, and flicked whatever was stuck to his finger into the air.

Jubie said, "Guess *he* was finding stuff!"

Early laughed, squeezing his arm. "You my man, Jubie! Come on, let's peek in the tutoring room."

Through the glass door, which was locked, they spied a bookshelf, a bunch of round tables with chairs, and some drawings on the wall.

"A dictionary in the corner!" Early said. "Two shelves of books! And look, a paper supplies cabinet — I need a notebook and a pen, so we're coming back here this afternoon. Maybe they'll let us borrow books and also give me something I can write in."

Jubie nodded. "I see games in the corner! Look over there, next to the paper cups. Spies always need games."

Next they headed up the stairs, past the open sleeping area with all the clusters, and up another flight to a floor with separate rooms. The linoleum and stairwells were chipped and worn everywhere; perhaps thousands had scuffed, kicked, and thumped their way through endless winters. The walls were bare. Every window was covered, and overhead bulbs were encased in wire, as if they might escape. Some of the doors, which were black metal, stood open.

Early whispered to Jubie, "Walk by as if you know where you're going, and look, but don't stare. You know, like you're not really paying attention."

Jubie frowned. "You're not the *boss* of me," he said. "Only Sum and Dash."

Early rolled her eyes. "I know — I'm just reminding you. Spies need to fit in. You want to be my finding buddy, don't you?"

"Yes." Jubie nodded.

"So," Early said.

They walked. Loud arguing came from behind one door, the sounds of a man and a woman, and at least two babies crying. Inside another room, boxes and open garbage bags were stacked floor to ceiling, clothes spilling outward in all directions. A TV was on in the corner. Sunlight from the one window filtered through a torn blue-and-white-striped curtain. The two bunk beds were unmade and blanketed with kids.

A boy just about Early's height peeked out of the next room, which was darker. "Hey!" he whispered. "You new here?"

"Yup," Early said.

The boy fell back inside as if pulled from behind, and a mom with tired eyes appeared. She didn't bother to say hello but glanced at Early and Jubie as if checking the weather, then told her son to stay on that floor. "And don't be wandering or I'll get my belt out. You know I mean it, now."

The boy said, "Yes, ma'am," and hopped out the door, giving Early a wink. "What're you doing?" he asked. "And why ain't you in school?" He had green, down-slanty eyes and smiled at Early as if he liked looking at her. She felt her face get warm.

"Why aren't *you*?" Early asked.

"Will be tomorrow. Sixth grade. We just moved back here, from another place where there was mice and my mom says she got itchy from the mattress."

"Oh," Jubie said. "I didn't like my mattress last night, neither. And there were people coughing and talking in our room."

"You'll get used to it" was the reply. "My name's Darren."

Early and Jubie introduced themselves. "So where's *your* dad?" Jubie asked. "Mine had mahhhney but he's lost right now. But we're peeking — *OW!* Whaddju do *that* for, Early?" Jubie's face crinkled up as he rubbed his arm where Early had just squeezed it.

"Be*cause*," she said fiercely. "Remember?"

Darren nodded. "I know! You're *spying*, right? Come on, I'll show you a few secrets. We've stayed here three or four times. They put us in this private room because my little brother snores and chokes all night." Shoving down on the loops of a too-short pair of jeans, he took off down the hall in a cheerful swagger. Odd tufts of hair boinged up here and there as if he'd had a trim with a pair of gardening shears.

"This here end of the hall you don't want to mess with — there's a real tough dad in that room, been at this shelter for a while, and I heard him yellin' last night. He's always burned about somethin'. Once saw him pick his little baby kid up by one foot and shake him.

"Now, over here, nice group, you can play with those kids. You'll see, you learn real quick which families to hang with, and when to be *real* busy when others go by, you know what I mean. Now here, there's a little girl got somethin' missing, but she's real sweet, all the kids are tellin' me. Wouldn't hurt a fly. When I go to a new shelter, I learn all the names, and get the good and bad guys figured out, you know? Never waste no time."

"I don't want those bad guys to find us again, Early! I'm scared!" Jubie began to cry.

"They can't come in here, Jubie. That's not what Darren meant. Right, Darren?" Early looked sideways at their new friend as if to say, *You'd better agree — tell you why later.*

Darren nodded. "I just meant *grumpy* folks, not shoe-rockin' evil."

"How many shelters have you stayed in?" Early asked. She wondered what *shoe rockin'* meant, and pictured a sneaker rolling back and forth on its sole.

Darren waved his hand. Early noticed a half-moon scar running along the back. Somehow, it looked good on him, like he was proud of it.

"Oh, a bunch," he was saying. "We're in and out. Sometimes we stay with one of my cousins until the ladies start fightin', then we go to the train station for a night or two, and once we took a bus to another city to stay with an uncle, but my mom, she has trouble keeping a job and taking care of us — costs so much to get a sitter — so we ended up back in Chicago. At least here she knows when the free days for exciting stuff are, where to get a meal, health stuff, all that. We don't have a home, but at least we got neighborhoods and places that we know. There's benches and parks that feel kinda homey, at least when it's not winter. And the last time she saw my dad, it was in Chicago, so just in case he wants to find us, she knows he'll look in the shelters here."

Early liked the way Darren made shelter life seem almost normal. "So dads know about the shelters?" she asked.

"You bet," Darren said.

"Yeah! Dads can find kids! Just like *we* see every little thing!" Jubie crowed happily.

Early nudged him, suddenly embarrassed by how young he sounded, but Darren didn't seem to mind. "I gotta head back before my mom starts swingin' leather," he said. "But maybe we'll catch you later this afternoon when the kids are out of school. There's a tutoring room downstairs — I was in there yesterday and those folks are all right. Plus sometimes they got a treat to share even if you don't got no homework."

"Yeah, I already wanted to go there," Early said, and stood up straighter. Darren straightened up, too, so they were eye to eye. "Hey, one quick question," Early added, wanting him to stay. "What was this building before it was a shelter?"

"Think it was a funeral parlor and then a chicken coop," Darren said, with a grin. Seeing Early's shocked expression, he said quickly, "Score! Naw, it was somethin' like a warehouse for pet food long time ago, and the place we eat downstairs was for the trucks. I asked the lady once. Later." He jerked his chin up in a quick salute, turned, and then spun back to say to Jubie, "Be easy, bro. Your sister rocks." Jubie shrugged and giggled. Early blushed. After Darren was gone, Jubie practiced turning away, bending, and then spinning back, just the way Darren had.

Lunch that day felt less strange than any of the other meals had been. The mom and baby who'd vanished in the ambulance weren't mentioned; there was grilled cheese, chips, grapes, and even chocolate graham crackers; and Early and Jubie told Sum they'd made a friend, pointing out Darren, who was busy helping his mom with his three little sisters, but still gave the Pearl kids a secretive nod.

Sum was cheerier because she'd gotten an appointment in two days to talk with a detective at the police department, someone who would surely listen to her suspicions.

"You and I will take the bus, Jubie, while Early's at her new school. And maybe that'll be when we get to the bottom of this crazy mess and get some traction on figuring out where your father might be. If we need to, we'll raise such a stink that someone official will have to uncover whatever bad stuff is going on. They'll find Dash, and when they do, he can set it all straight. Then all of this will just feel like a bad dream. Funny what a difference one successful phone connection can make!"

Although happy to hear her mom sounding so bubbly and hopeful, the thought of school made Early's heart drop. Closing her eyes, she sent her dad a message.

Hurry up and come home, Dash! Gotta go to a new school, and I don't want to. I've had enough of all this.

She opened her eyes to see Darren looking at her, with no winks but a tiny, questioning smile. She rubbed one eye, as if there were something stuck in there, and straightened her ponytail. Noticing her sneakers were untied, she bent over to fix them, then watched her brother eat. She waited for Dash's voice in her head, but all she heard was the sound of Jubie chewing his second cookie with his mouth open, chewing and humming.

Thinking she wanted a bite, he clutched it protectively against his shirt. When Early didn't react, Jubie held the half-eaten cookie over one eye and whispered, "Spies!" then popped the rest into his mouth and grinned.

Early looked back toward Darren, but he was gone. She wished she'd returned his smile.

Circle, *from the Middle English* cercle *and the Latin* circulus

Noun: a flat curve that is always and forever equidistant from a given fixed point; a group of people sharing an interest or activity.

Verb: to enclose, revolve, move around an object without reaching or touching it.

Circle

"Aisha."

"Chantuse."

"Key."

"Raven."

"Gani."

"Nando."

Early lost track of the names; the kids stood in a circle inside the tutoring room, and Mr. John, a young man with a white button-down shirt and jeans, introduced them all. He then clapped his hands and said, "Okay! Who's got homework to do before we play a few games?"

Jubie held tight to Early's hand and neither moved. Other kids unzipped backpacks and pulled out work sheets. In the middle of each of the tables was a jelly jar with pencils. A sign on the jar said HELP YOURSELF IF YOU NEED TO. PLEASE SHARPEN PENCIL BEFORE RETURNING IT.

"I'm not in my new school yet," Early explained to Mr. John, when he asked if he could help her get started. "But I will be, the day after tomorrow. Could my brother and I look at some of your books? And — well, my notebook is gone, and do you have a small one I could write in?"

"Yeah," Jubie piped up, before the tutor could answer. "Those bad guys took everything, and smashed all of our dishes and stuff, too. Pushed my mom and she fell down. They should be in jail. Or *pow*! Dead!"

Early's heart sank. Keeping secrets was not her brother's strong point. She felt her face getting hot as the other kids looked up from the tables. The room was suddenly quiet.

Jubie, standing up straighter, added, "And Early and I are gonna be *spies*."

One of the older boys patted a chair next to him and said, "Here, spy dude, you can come sit next to me. We got paper and crayons you can use for your work."

Sliding happily into the chair, Jubie grabbed a large red crayon and began to draw squashed circles, one inside the other. He didn't seem to notice the other kids smiling at him.

The tutor was digging in the supplies closet. "We used to have some small notebooks that one of the volunteers brought in . . . wait, no, darn!" He turned back to Early and shrugged.

"If you got some scissors, I can help her make one," offered one of the girls. Terrible pink scars covered her neck, as if someone had ironed wrinkles onto her skin. She wore a spotless yellow sweater with a velvety collar, one Early would have loved to have. Her dozens of hair clips each boasted a perfect bow, and she touched them once in a while, as if to be sure they were still in place.

"You can call me Aisha," the girl said to Early, and ducked her chin down toward her collarbone. "It says *Belinda* on my papers, but I renamed myself."

Soon the two were cheerfully folding and cutting and stapling, and Early had a homemade pocket notebook. "Thanks so much!" she said with a grin. Meeting Aisha was one of the best things that had happened since leaving home. The other was Darren. Early wondered why he hadn't come to the tutoring room yet.

"Do you like to read books?" Early asked as they carefully lined up the edges of each sheet of paper.

"Not too good at it," her new friend replied. "It's kinda hard, you know?"

"I could help you," Early said. "It's so fun, like seeing a movie with popcorn, only better, because it stays in your head as long as you want it to and then you can go back and see parts of it again!"

Aisha looked at her and shrugged. Her lower lip went out. "You sound like a teacher."

Early wished she hadn't been so quick to share. A teacher! This was no compliment. Was that because she said she liked reading? Would Aisha still be her friend if she knew how much everyone in the Pearl family loved books?

She tried to explain. "Books can keep you company, just like a stuffed animal or doll. My dad, we call him Dash, makes us kids hungry for words and stories. My mom loves 'em, too. And Jubie there can't read, but he likes to listen. Plus, we don't have a TV and you never get bored if you can read. There's lots of free libraries in Chicago and anyone can take out books whenever they want. Just walk in, wave your card, and walk out with whole worlds under one arm, not even a penny spent! That's what my dad used to say. What kind of stuff do you like to do?"

Aisha sat up straight for the first time. "Well, I want to have my own hair salon one day. And I like to play with dolls, except my favorite, Chocolate Cake, fell out a window and is gone. Got *pushed* out a window." Her eyes filled with tears and she blinked rapidly.

"Yeah, all my favorite things are gone, too," Early said. "All but one old book. Losing stuff stinks."

Aisha looked at her gratefully. "Yeah. I think sometimes the grown-ups don't get how much our things matter. Plus we lost our home."

"Us, too." Early nodded. "That feels superbad."

The other kids at the table nodded. "How you spell your name?" one boy at the table asked. "That's one crazy name — I like it!"

"E-A-R-L-Y, like the opposite of *late*, and our last name is Pearl."

"Ooh, that's real pretty!"

"Que lindo."

"Nice sounding, like a movie star!"

"Uh-*huh*, real smooth!"

Suddenly Early felt like she belonged, at least a tiny bit.

"And my real name's Jubilation," blurted Jubie. "It means loud! And cheerful!"

"That's a church-goin' kinda name, isn't it?" another boy asked.

Jubie looked at his sister for help. Early shrugged, saying, "I dunno — we only go to church a couple times a year, but I know my parents liked the word, you know? They think a word or a name can be worth noticing. Like it's free but valuable."

"That's what my grandma says," another girl piped up. "You want to be *remembered*."

The other kids nodded, and suddenly Early and Jubie were inside a circle.

After she and Aisha finished two more pocket notebooks, Early tried to get her new friend to keep one, but she didn't want it. "I'd waste it," she explained.

Early took Jubie over to look at the books, on the side of the room. Most seemed brand-new, as if they'd never been opened. She asked Mr. John if she and Jubie could each borrow a book, and when the tutor hesitated, Early made two homemade library cards, one for her and one for her brother. She wrote *Treasure Island* and the date on the bottom of hers, and *The Lion King* on the bottom of Jubie's.

"We'll bring them back soon," she promised.

The other kids watched, and although no one else asked to borrow a book, no one said anything nasty, either.

On the way out, hugging the homemade notebooks, a pencil, and the two borrowed books, Early felt sad that shoe-rockin' Darren hadn't made it. She asked if anyone had seen him that afternoon. The other kids looked blank.

One shrugged as he zipped up his backpack. "Sometimes a family gets pulled out and sent to another shelter, *bang!* and there's no warning. Or something happens to one of the older boys who weren't allowed to stay here, and the mom makes the whole family move. *Dang!* We're draggin' those Hefty garbage bags again. This here's a tough life," he said.

Mr. John reached over and patted him on the shoulder. "But we're here for you guys," he said.

"That don't always do much good," the kid said, turning away. Early's heart sank. *What's the rhythm, Langston?* she asked in her head. *What's the rhythm?* Suddenly she felt lost.

As they left the tutoring room, she looked at the clock. It was 4:44. A shiver raced down her spine, and she reached for Jubie's hand.

Circle

"Presto! A wall, our own light, a wild reading corner, and a laundry line!" Sum swept her arm out and bowed, as if stepping into their cluster was a special event.

While Early and Jubie had been in the tutoring room, Sum had hunted through a new load of donations that had arrived at the shelter. Out popped a sheet covered with clouds, a battery-powered flashlight, and a new pink-and-orange pillow with a zebra-skin pattern, one big enough for all three Pearls to lean against. She'd tidied up, adding the sheet as a wall and hanging their clean underwear to dry on a bathrobe tie stretched between the upper bunks. Things looked almost homey.

Darren and his family weren't at dinner that night. After eating, the three Pearls did sit-ups and stretches in the second-floor hallway, as they hadn't left the shelter since they'd arrived the day before. Then they showered, brushed their teeth, and cuddled in the lower bunk while Sum read *Treasure Island*, Early on one side and Jubie on the other.

Dash had already read it aloud to the family, skipping parts that were confusing or too scary, so it was more or less familiar. They tried to ignore the other sounds in the room, until a cough, right behind Sum's head, on the other side of the cloud sheet, made her sit up straight and bang her head on the top bunk.

"Yeow! Second time I've done that! Who's out there?" She jerked the sheet aside, and there were four faces — three girls and a boy — all sitting on their knees, listening.

"See? You stupid!" the oldest said, swatting at the youngest, who had a terribly runny nose. He started to cry, which made the coughing worse.

Saying, "Keep our place," to Early, Sum went around the side of the bed and asked the kids where their mom was. They pointed. She walked over, bent to talk to a woman lying down on a lower bunk with a baby, and came back smiling. "She says you can listen," Sum said to the kids, her voice soft.

She beckoned and they followed, stepping on one another in their eagerness to get into the Pearls' cluster. When she patted a lower bunk, all four obediently sat down. She handed the littlest boy a piece of toilet paper to blow his nose.

"Please wash your hands afterward," she murmured. "We'll wait for you." The boy trotted off to do as she'd said, and as soon as he was settled back on the bed, Sum explained that the book was about pirates and added, "Okay, we're going back a couple of pages, so you don't miss the beginning.

"This is happening over two hundred years ago, and it's about looking for stolen treasure. And parts of it, I have to warn you, are about too much alcohol, murder, and mean, scary men. Stop me if it gets too frightening; I don't want to give anyone bad dreams! But it *is* a great story. It's being told by a boy who lives in a small guesthouse run by his parents, by the seashore in England. That's on the other side of the Atlantic Ocean. The boy has to help out a lot; he doesn't have it too easy."

The four visitors nodded, and the oldest girl said, "Is it, like, X-rated?"

"Well." Sum paused. "I think it's okay for us. It's been around for many generations and people all over the world have grown up reading it."

"Go, Sum!" Jubie said impatiently. Early thought Darren would like hearing this scary story, one told by a young boy. Too bad he couldn't be here, too.

Sum began, in an unhurried, listen-to-each-word voice:

"I remember him as if it were yesterday, as he came plodding to the inn door, his sea-chest following behind him in a hand-barrow; a tall, strong, heavy, nut-brown man; his tarry pigtail falling over the shoulders of his soiled blue coat, his hands ragged and scarred, with black, broken nails; and the sabre cut across one cheek, a dirty, livid white. I remember him looking

round the cove and whistling to himself as he did so, and then breaking out in that old sea-song that he sang so often afterwards:

'Fifteen men on the dead man's chest —

Yo-ho-ho and a bottle of rum!'

in the high, old tottering voice that seemed to have been tuned and broken at the capstan bars. Part of a ship," Sum explained. *"Then he rapped on the door with a bit of stick like a handspike that he carried, and when my father appeared, called roughly for a glass of rum. This, when it was brought to him, he drank slowly, like a connoisseur, lingering on the taste, and still looking about him at the cliffs and up at our signboard.*

" 'This is a handy cove,' says he, at length, 'and a pleasant sittyated grog-shop.' That means a bar," said Sum. *" 'Much company, mate?'*

"My father told him no, very little company, the more was the pity.

" 'Well, then,' said he, 'this is the berth for me.' A berth is a bed on a ship," Sum explained. *" 'Here you, matey,' he cried to the man who trundled the barrow; 'bring up alongside and help up my chest.'* A sea chest was what they used for a suitcase in those days. It looked like a treasure chest and sometimes *was*! *'I'll stay here a bit,' he continued. 'I'm a plain man; rum and bacon and eggs is what I want. . . . Oh, I see what you're at — there,' and he threw down three or four gold pieces on the threshold. 'You can tell me when I've worked through that,' says he, looking as fierce as a commander."*

Sum went on to read about the pirate bullying everyone at the house for the next few weeks, telling terrible stories about *"some of the wickedest men that God ever allowed upon the sea,"* and then demanding to be fed and taken care of, but without more pay. He was too frightening to refuse. Plus, he never bathed or washed his clothes, and as he had arrived in rags, he was looking pretty bad. He kept his sea chest, which he hinted was filled with valuables, locked at all times. Sum also read about the pirate telling the young boy to keep a *"weather-eye open,"* meaning to look out all the time, for a *"sea-faring man with one leg."* It was clear that the pirate was worried about this man.

"And here I'll stop," Sum said. "Hope it isn't too much. Just fiction, you know!"

One of the kids on the bunk said, "Where's the man's home?"

Sum looked sideways at the kids and sighed. "Probably hadn't had one for years. Maybe never. I'll bet he just lived on ships when he went out to sea."

"Must've smelled sumpin awful!" another kid said. "As bad as that guy who lives in the doorway down the street. Once we said hi to him when he was shaking out his sleeping bag, and *peeee-uw!*"

"Poor soul," Sum said.

"I could live on a ship!" the boy with the runny nose said, his voice high with excitement. "And have a sea chest! With my stuff inside!"

"No toilets or running water," Sum said. "Lotta rats and bugs. Worms in the food. No toilet paper."

"Aw, *nasty*!"

"Pirates didn't got it easy!"

"Pirates don't work, they just steal, right?" asked Jubie. "So they don't get a home. They're *baaaaad*!"

"Sometimes bad people get homes and good people don't,"

Sum said lightly. "We'll find out who gets what if we keep reading. Off you go, kids."

That night, with the three Pearls still curled into one bunk, Early hoped Dash wasn't being bullied, wherever he was.

Good night, Dash, she said, in her mind. *Sweet dreams. We're working hard to find you. But I have a question: What does 4:44 mean? Did you make me see it today?*

I remember what you wrote in your notebook, the last page, about the times. If 4 + 4 + 4 = 12, and 1 + 2 = 3, is 3 a clue? Or is it just that when you add and re-add those lines of repeating numbers, they turn into a rhythm of 3, 6, 9 and that's what matters? But why?

I don't like 3. We Pearls are a 4, not a 3, and I don't want to notice 3s! I wish something in your notebook had added up to 4.

Tears rolled off into the pillow under Early's cheek. And then she felt it: Dash's hand cupping the side of her head, just a light touch, the way he did at home, checking on her and Jubie before he and Sum went to sleep. She felt it!

Her eyes popped open, and she sat up on one elbow. Sum's back was to her, and Jubie was curled against Sum. Sum turned her head.

"You doing okay, Early?" Her voice was sleepy.

Early knew she couldn't tell what had just happened, not without making Sum sad. She forced some cheerfulness into her voice. "Yeah, night."

When she'd settled back on the pillow, she whispered in her head, *Thanks, Dash.*

She lay awake for what felt like ages, listening to the murmurs and occasional crying, sneezing, and sniffling in the big room. Snow with a steady wind made *plitt-plitt-pishhhh* sounds against the windows, and every once in a while a radiator wheezed steam. The guard in the corner read a magazine with a flashlight and occasionally walked the length of the room and back, one of her sneakers squeaking under her weight. Each time someone tiptoed by to the bathroom, he or she crossed the light in the open door, dragging a panel of shadow across Early's face, first one way and then the other.

Who could help them?

And then, suddenly, she remembered a name. Someone from Dash's past, someone who might still be around. She tucked the thought beneath her pillow.

"I can do this, Dash," she whispered.

ℯℯℯ

Circle

Early opened to the first page of one of her new notebooks and wrote, each letter spy-style neat: *Find Skip Waive, Dash's old teacher. Check telephone book first.*

By midmorning, she felt ready to try the new school, *more* than ready. Time dragged, the hands on the shelter clocks seeming barely to move.

Early and Jubie walked by the room Darren had been in, but it was quiet, *too* quiet. He might be in school, but then where were his mom and the littler kids? They hadn't been at breakfast this morning. Early sighed, and wondered if she'd ever see Darren again.

The tutoring room was locked and empty until three o'clock, when the bigger kids came back from school. Early hoped there was a phone book in there; she could do this on her own. She'd tell Sum when she had good news to share.

Her mother spent what seemed like endless hours waiting in the phone lines, hoping to be prepared for her trip to the police station the next day by getting free legal advice ahead of time. Most of the places she reached forced her to leave a message giving her name and the main number of the shelter, and she'd been told those calls hardly ever got returned. She also met with the shelter employment counselor, who wanted a promise that she'd put Jubie into affordable day care before she was offered a job, something she and Dash had agreed they wouldn't do with their kids. Not that there was much work around, these days, for people who'd only finished high school! Sum was in no mood to sympathize with Early and Jubie's feeling bored.

Early had read *The Lion King* to her brother three times when Jubie found another boy to play with up in the sleeping area, a kid who'd been wandering around the edges of the room. Early breathed a sigh of relief. She'd just picked up her notebook again when Jubie was back.

"He pulled my shirt, Early!" Jubie whined. "He's not being nice, and we got nothing fun to play with! Just his little sister's baby toys."

Early sighed. "Come on, we'll play red-light-green-light in the hall." As soon as they started, more kids about Jubie's age showed up. Early explained the rules. Soon she had ten small people looking at her.

She turned her back and covered her eyes. "Green light . . ." she said, then spun around. "Red!" This went on with one four- or five-year-old after another becoming the leader until someone gave an earsplitting shriek and a guard came out and told them all to quiet down.

"You-all running a play group here," the guard said. "You somebody's good daughter," she added, and patted Early on the shoulder.

That helped. Early went on to organize a game of statues, which was quieter, and then a game of telephone, in which the kids sat in a circle and each whispered a name in the next ear. She was exhausted by the time lunch rolled around and Sum came downstairs.

Her mother looked thunderous right when Early wanted her to smile and give her a hug. "I took care of a lot of kids while you were up there," Early began.

"That's good," Sum said, in a flat voice. "Wish I'd done something that worthwhile."

Lunch was icky, greasy meat with green noodles on the side. Jubie was whining again. Early started to feel desperate. "Couldn't you take us out for a little walk, Sum?" she asked. "Wouldn't it feel good to see the sky and get some air?"

Sum looked blankly at her daughter. "Yeah, but I need every minute I have to find out what our rights are before I sit down with those police people again. I gotta make this appointment tomorrow count, you know?" Then, as if seeing Early's unhappy face for the first time, she said, "I'm sorry, baby. It'll feel refreshing to get to school tomorrow, and if you can just keep an eye on Jubie for a few more hours, that'll be the best help ever."

Early nodded numbly. She thought of all the fun things they'd had at home — Play-Doh, paints and crayons, paper, toys . . . and, of course, books. They'd gone on trips to the local library, sometimes twice a week. Made cookies with Sum. Had blocks and Legos to build with. It had all felt normal then, but so much choice now seemed like luxury.

Circle

Early spread her clothes carefully on one of the bunks and ironed them with the palm of her hand. She got a sock from the dirty laundry, wet it, and cleaned the sides of her sneakers. Once dressed, she sat quietly on the bed and wrote in her new notebook, *Hoping for hope today.* She paused and looked up. Sum was watching, her eyes gentle and like-old-times warm. Tears suddenly prickled in Early's eyes, and she turned her head.

"Love you, Early Pearl," her mother whispered.

Early got busy putting her notebook away and blinked like mad before answering, "Yeah, me, too, Sum."

Sum and Jubie were downstairs when Early left with a group of twelve kids to go to school that morning with Mrs. Happadee. No other parents were there to see them off. Sum stepped up and tied Early's scarf extra tight around her face. "Cold out there, now!" she said. "You keep those gloves on, too."

Early nodded.

"Your mom's real nice," Aisha said as they stepped outside. "Mine's always been tired. Sometimes we kids had to call her lots to get her up for breakfast. Before here."

Early nodded again. Weird, she hadn't *seen* any other kids at mealtimes with Aisha and her mom. "There's other kids in your family?" Early asked.

Aisha tucked her chin deeper into her scarf. "They died in the fire, with my grandma," she said. "Used to be. Just me and my mom now."

Whoa. Early looked sideways at Aisha. "I'm sorry — that's so, so sad. I didn't know."

Aisha shrugged, then coughed. "It happened three years ago now, when I was little. I'll always miss them. Sometimes I hear their voices in my head. We got their pictures with us, wherever we go. And my mom's still real upset. Every time she gets a job, like restaurant-counter work, a few weeks go by and then they want her to leave. Maybe because she cries real easy, I'm not sure." Aisha wiped her nose on the back of her mitten.

"Your mom seems nice," Early said, not knowing what else to say. *Sometimes I hear their voices in my head.* Early especially hated that part of Aisha's story.

They walked a little without talking, boots crunching in the snow. It was a gray morning, no wind, and the neighborhood looked bigger and busier than Woodlawn. It also seemed like there were a lot of very poor people out on the streets. Some held coffee cups with jingly change in them, saying things like "Good morning, can you help the homeless? Have a blessed day." Others huddled over grates on the sidewalk, heads down, feet wrapped in thick rags for warmth.

Some had hand-lettered cardboard signs that read *I am Hungry. Lost my Home. Fallen down in Hard Times.* Or, *I am a Vietnam Vet with injuries. I fought for you! Can you give back to me? I have four grandkids to raise and no work.* Or, *Lost my job. Got medical bills I can't pay. Please help me stay alive. Don't want to die.* Others simply walked, wandering back and forth, talking to no one Early could see. She wished she had some coins to give. Seeing these people out in the cold, many trying to share their stories while no one listened, made Early move slower and slower. Didn't anyone care? Aisha pulled on her arm.

Mrs. Happadee glanced back, then said, "Early, come on up here. I want to tell you a few things about your new school. You'll love it! Now, this morning they'll be giving you some tests to see what grade you should go into, so you'll be in the office most of the day. But you can have lunch with the other kids, so keep an eye out for Aisha here."

"I'll look for her," Aisha piped up.

"But I'm in fifth grade. They can call my old school and ask."

"Well, they just like to do things this way, so that's what'll happen. Don't worry, it'll be fine."

"And, Mrs. Happadee?" Early glanced at her face.

"Yes?"

"Did Darren, ah, leave the shelter? He kinda made friends with me and Jubie. . . ."

Mrs. Happadee sighed. "Very sad. A friend of his mom's died and they all left suddenly, but, well, I have a feeling they'll be back."

"Not his dad?"

"Nooo, not his dad." Mrs. Happadee's tone made it clear the conversation was over.

When they stepped inside the door, the other kids walked down the hall in a little cluster. The school was big and gloomy, as if someone had forgotten to turn on the lights. A woman in a security uniform sat at a desk at the entrance, calling hello to some of the kids by name. Army-green lockers lined the halls, and kids put away backpacks and boots with the familiar *whack-thud-slam* that echoes through most schools at the beginning of each day.

Mrs. Happadee ushered Early into an office down the hall. "New student," she called out. "Early Pearl, she's registered."

"Gotcha. What a pretty name," a woman with a blond beehive hairdo cooed. She walked long lemon-striped nails back and forth over a stack of papers. "I'll be right with you. Oh! You need breakfast, sugar?"

Early shook her head. "No, ma'am," she said. As soon as the beehive left the room, Early looked around, skimming the shelves for a telephone book.

A new one lay just behind the reception area.

Before starting the test, several minutes later, Early asked if she could have the phone book next to her, just in case she wanted to sit on it.

"Well, why not," the beehive lady said, and brought it over.

That wasn't so hard, Early thought to herself. She was getting used to the life of a spy.

The test was all true-false questions. Early filled in little round circles with her pencil, turning page after page. Soon the bell rang for lunch, and she heard kids pouring out into the hall.

"Can I go?" she asked.

"Soon as you're done" was the reply.

Early hustled through the last couple of pages. "That was pretty easy. Oh, and can I just look up a family friend, as long as this phone book is here?" she asked.

"Certainly. Let me have the test. Right back, honey." The lady left the room, coffee mug in hand, test under one elbow.

Early thumbed through the *W*'s, her heart beginning to pound. *Oh, please, Mr. Waive, be here,* she thought. Her finger ran down the column, but there was no *Waive* with an *i* in the spelling. Dash had told her that it was an unusual Irish name. She slapped the book shut, suddenly discouraged.

The beehive lady returned, steam rising from her mug, and smiled pleasantly. "Find it?" she asked.

"Well, no." Early took a deep breath and added, "You see, my dad's disappeared, and we're pretty sure he got caught in something bad. I want to get in touch with his old teacher, Mr. Skip Waive. I know he taught in a school on the South Side. He was good to my dad and he might be able to help us."

"Know which school?" the lady asked brightly.

"No." Early frowned. "Isn't there a teacher list you could look at?"

"Not really, but I'll see what I can do. You just stop by again after lunch."

"Oh, thank you, Mrs. —" Early paused.

"B.," the woman said, smiling.

Early hurried away, wanting to laugh. A Mrs. B. with a hairdo for bees on her head and yellow stripes on her dark fingernails! She felt almost bouncy walking into the lunchroom.

Yikes. As the door swung shut behind her, she stopped dead. The room was huge, and filled with kids, talking and laughing and eating. She scanned the faces. No Aisha, at least that she could see. She walked slowly toward the line for food, watching carefully so that when she grabbed her tray and fork and spoon, she'd look like she knew what she was doing.

Meat loaf . . . potatoes . . . peas . . . a dish with applesauce. Early paused, holding her tray, and started to sit at a table that was half full when a girl at the other end, with a group of boys, called, "No room! Holding seats!" then covered a smile with her hand.

Early glanced at her face and turned away, trying to look like she didn't care. She tried another table, this one all girls. No one there told her not to sit, but they didn't make her welcome, either; those sitting closest turned their backs. She ate quietly, each mouthful taking forever to chew, studying the napkin holder in front of her.

As she stood to go, she didn't know what to do with her tray. "Over there." A girl with long, perfect braids pointed to the corner. "That's where garbage goes." She then tossed her head, a black braid snaking backward over one shoulder.

"Thanks," Early said. Now the girl was pressing one finger under her nose, as if she smelled something bad.

"Stinkin' shelter kids," she hissed, in a loud voice to her friend. "Give our school a bad name. My mom says not to talk to 'em, but I'm not that unkind."

Early couldn't breathe for a moment. *Shelter kids!* She glared at the girl, her eyes filling with tears, then wished she hadn't. The girl made her eyes big and round and gave Early a what-did-*I*-do look. Her friends backed her up, wrinkling noses. "Hey, I can't take the unwashed clothes, can you, Marie?" one asked, and the group stood together, turned, and walked away.

Early stumbled toward the corner with her tray and shoved it hard onto the pile. She pictured whizzing it expertly at the girl's head, and bits of gravy and potato going everywhere — the group of girls screaming, their clean, smooth T-shirts spotted with grease.

When Early got back to the office, Mrs. B. said, "Well, I have some nice news for you. I've found Mr. Waive. He's retired, and I need permission from him before I can give you his phone number. Can you spell your dad's first name for me?"

Early did, her misery lifting. "Sounds like the mystery writer Dashiell Hammett. Ooh, thank you so much!"

"Never heard of him, but that's nice, you're a bookish family," Mrs. B. said. "I don't read much, gotta admit," she giggled, as if that were adorable.

"My dad works in the big Chicago Public Library downtown, in Harold Washington. His department is History and Social Sciences," Early said.

"Ahh," Mrs. B. cooed, just as if Early had said she loved giant cupcakes. "Well, I can tell you're a special daughter, and I'll see what I can do. You be sure to stop by and see me tomorrow. Meanwhile, where would you like to wait? I'm assuming you're walking back with Mrs. Happadee after school today."

Early spent the rest of the afternoon in the library with some of her old friends. She reread the part in Katherine Paterson's *The Great Gilly Hopkins* in which Gilly snipped off a hunk of her own hair, did everything possible to make everyone around her angry, and started a huge, bloody fight at school, even staring down the principal when she got sent to his office.

Early imagined chopping off one of those long, excellent braids and getting thrown out of the Hughes School before she'd even started. And what if she complained and moaned about taking care of Jubie and comforting Sum? About listening, all the time, with every bit of her aching soul, for Dash? She was *tired* of trying to make things better. *Tired* of putting a good spin on things. Tired.

Then she thought about the people on the street, the ones no one even seemed to notice. That sadness blotted up some of her anger at the unfairness of it all. What had happened to their family might be unjust and frightening, but at least they had things to eat and stuff to do. At least people listened to what she had to say. At least Sum would get help from the police once they understood that Dash hadn't done anything wrong. At least they had hope.

As they lined up to walk back to Helping Hand, Aisha rushed over. "Where were you, Early? I looked and looked!"

"Maybe the later lunch crowd," Mrs. Happadee suggested. "By the way, Early, I understand you're going in with the fifth grade tomorrow. You did fine on the test."

"That's good," Early said, her voice flat. "Yeah, I looked for you, too, Aisha. Sat with some mean kids. They said I smelled bad because I came from the shelter."

"Aw, that's terrible!" Mrs. Happadee scowled. "Well, you just ignore those kind of comments. Obnoxious! They don't know any better."

"Yes, ma'am," Early said. She pictured that lovely braid on the lunchroom floor, surrounded by squashed peas, crumbs, and sticky sneaker prints.

On the way home, she nodded hello to each person who was

begging on the street. The generous response she got, a whole lot of "Bless you, darlin', good luck, now!" and "Know you'd help if you could," made her feel more like herself. Like Dash's girl.

That is, until she saw Sum waiting inside the door of Helping Hand, Jubie in her arms, pacing as tears ran down her face.

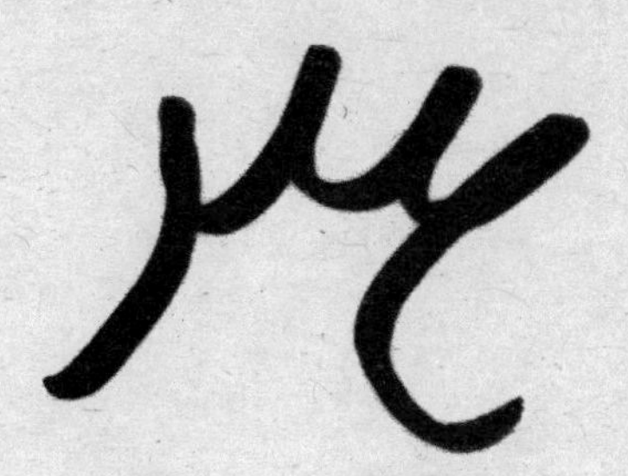

Crimp, *from the Dutch* krimpen

Verb: to make wavy or add a wrinkly pattern; to fold or bend stiff leather or metal; to pinch or crease in order to seal, as around the rim of a piecrust.

Noun: an addition that causes a problem; an unwanted wrinkle.

Crimp

Mrs. Happadee hurried the Pearl family into her office, *cluck-clucking* and *now-nowing* down a long hallway, and left them there with a box of tissues. "We all need a few minutes of privacy sometimes," she said, and gently shut the door.

Sum's and Early's stories spilled and ran together, blurring and bending all their "hold fasts" and hopeful words. Jubie had fallen asleep on Sum's shoulder, so they could talk freely.

"You first," Sum began. She hated Early's lunchroom story. "I'm so sorry this has happened to you, baby. Dash would feel terrible, too. One day it'll be a tale to tell."

And Early sure hated Sum's story.

When Sum and Jubie arrived at the police station that morning, they were shown into a room with three officers, two of them detectives. Sum was told immediately that there was a warrant out for Dash's arrest and the FBI was now involved.

"Thanks for coming in — you saved us a trip," one of the men said, his face twisting into an unfunny smile.

"What?" Sum had wailed. "You're *smiling* at me? What kind of nightmare is this? I thought I was coming to you folks for help!"

Sum then told Early the bad news. First, Mr. Pincer had told the detectives that no one by the name of Al worked on the sixth floor at Harold Washington and that there was no bookseller, international or not, by the name of Lyman Scrub. He didn't exist. Second, this supervisor asked why anyone honest at the Chicago Public Library would ever be involved with selling books that valuable on the side, or having them shipped to his home in the process.

"Whoa," Early whispered.

Sum went on, "And that's when I started to see red. I said, 'And what if my husband didn't realize that this book business was illegal, if it even *was*? What if he trusted this person Al, who, believe me, does exist. Or what if Al is a made-up name for a Library Page at History and Social Sciences, for someone who's been breaking the law but wanted my husband to take the blame? For someone who's still there? And is it my husband's fault if this Lyman Scrub person, the one who organized the whole thing, put a crimp in the works by using a fake name?'

"'We can —' an officer began, but I told him, 'And has everyone forgotten that a group of three men and a woman, folks with pale skin and a full-body disguise, pushed me to the ground, threatened our eleven-year-old daughter, and destroyed our apartment? They stole my wallet, our books, and a bunch of family notebooks. Does that not matter here? What happened to the laws that protect the innocent?'"

Sum shook her head as she told Early, "The officer continued smoothly, as if I'd only sneezed, 'We are hoping your husband turns himself in and can clear his name.'"

"Whoa," Early said again.

Sum held up her hand. "Just wait. Here's the slammer: One of the officers then asked me about jewelry. I told him that Dash and I only had wedding bands, and that they weren't expensive gold. I showed him my hand.

"'No engagement ring?' the officer asked.

"'We couldn't afford it,' I said. 'We've been saving all these years for a home.'

"The officer reached in a metal box sitting on the table and pulled out something tiny and held it up to the light. It sparkled. 'Ever seen this before?' he asked me.

"'Is it a *diamond*?' I asked, squinting for a better look.

"'Yes, small, but quite valuable: a stone probably cut for an engagement ring. But this is no ordinary stone. Using a laser to identify it, a jeweler in Chicago tells us this is a gemstone from *the biggest diamond heist in history*. The theft happened almost eight years ago, in the European city of Antwerp, in Belgium. Only one of the other thousands of stones taken that day has been recovered. This is the second. Giant news.'"

"So he was just trying to impress you or something?" Early asked.

Sum paused. "That's what I was wondering, too, and then Jubie blurted, 'I *love* Belgian waffles! Yeah, cream and syrup, sticky-wicky fingers!' and suddenly I didn't know if I was laughing or crying.

"The detective glared at me and said, 'You won't be smiling when you hear the next part. Sticky is right. *This stone was found on the floor in your apartment* when the police went through the mess again. One of the officers picked it up next to the broken coffee table.'"

Sum paused and blew her nose. "I asked them right away if someone could've gotten in there and dropped the diamond to make Dash look bad. They ignored me. And, of course, finding the stolen gemstone is what sealed the arrest warrant and made the whole darn book business look so bad. This is all just one thousand percent insane."

Early was stunned. "Dash would never *steal* for us, would he?" she whispered.

"Of course not, baby. Never."

Early could only nod, the dreadfulness of this whole day catching up to her.

Sum was still talking, her voice now shaking. "I realized something awful in that room today. That when you're this poor and without money or an address, hardly anyone thinks you're worth listening to or helping. Just the words *living in a shelter* make you someone the police aren't too worried about, less than your average citizen when it comes to rights. And now that Dash is missing, the fact that he'd been a man with a job, a family, and a home doesn't seem to count. Seeing how excited the detectives were about that dumb diamond today, I knew they cared more about the stone than the man. Or us."

"Dang," Early said, swallowing hard. "That's scary." Her voice wobbled. "Dash is gonna be okay, right, Sum?"

"Of course, baby," Sum said softly. Then she shook her head and sat up straighter, as if to pull them all together.

Jubie, now awake, said, "Pow, pow! Let's get those guys!"

"Oh, Lord, don't talk like that," Sum said. "Seriously, son, you're hearing an awful lot these days and you need to stay quiet and polite in all of this. No gun talk. Don't want to make extra trouble for Dash."

Sum reached for her children's hands so the three made a circle. She went on, "And before Jubie and I left today, one of the policemen told me that I shouldn't talk to anyone about the diamond, not yet. So, you two, you know what that means: Zip the lip."

"Okay," Early said slowly. "But why did they talk about it in front of Jubie, then?"

"He's four," Sum said.

"Zip the lip," Jubie promised, nodding so hard and fast, his teeth rattled. "Ow," he added, popping a finger in his mouth.

"Understand, son? Not a word about what we heard today."

"I'll be good." Jubie nodded.

"Hey," Early said. "I was saving this for later, but . . . I did think of one person who might help us, Sum. Remember Dash talking about Mr. Waive? Well, he's got a cell phone number. I asked a lady in the office at school today to look him up in a Chicago Public Schools directory. She's getting in touch to let him know that I'm Dash's daughter, and to ask if I can call."

Sum reached over and pulled Early's head against her body. "Well, who knows. You never give up, do you?" she said, and hugged her daughter so long and hard that the zipper on her sweatshirt made a little print on Early's cheek.

That evening the three Pearls ate without talking, even Jubie. After dinner, as happened every Thursday evening, the shelter showed a movie against one wall in the main room. Anyone who wanted to watch could sit at the tables in the eating area. It was *Peter Pan*, an old version.

The audience was quiet, happy to watch Tinker Bell, the flying lesson, and later on, the pirates. The story of Peter, the spunky boy without a home. The Lost Boys. It seemed like everyone in the shelter had come downstairs.

And that night, after the three Pearls had gone to sleep and a rising moon slipped rosy light between broken slats in the shelter blinds, Early had a bizarre dream.

Crimp

"Psst! Early, wake up!"

Dash is leaning over her in the bunk, his fingers to his lips. She startles awake and reaches to hug him, a sob rising in her throat, but he steps back. Smiling, he says, "I'm setting you and Sum and Jubie free, out of reach!"

"But how, Dash? Oh, I'm so glad you're home!"

"That's the problem. I can't come home, not yet. We don't have one. Gotta figure that out. Have to research rhythms."

"Oh, but you know we will, Dash, you know one day we'll all head home, like you always promised. You *know* we will!"

"You can do it. You got everything you need." He takes another step back.

"Why can't you stay here with us, Dash? Please! You can't leave us again!"

As Dash melts into shadow, his finger to his lips, Early realizes the four of them are suddenly outside the shelter and standing in the street. She isn't cold. Turning her head with an effort, as if against pressure, she sees that Jubie and Sum aren't really awake; they don't know where they are and can't see Dash.

Dash is speaking. "I'm going to show you how to fly. Raise your arms, and you'll feel the strength come from a bright circle right in the center of your body. I'll see you at H-O-M-E. Just say the *O* in the middle, and up you go. O . . . O . . ."

Suddenly the three are up in the air, arms out in front, and Early can feel the lift, the hope, and the wind. Somehow, she knows that Sum and Jubie are with her and that she's doing what Dash wants her to do.

The city below twinkles, hums, and grinds. Here a car is honking; there, an ambulance speeds through a red light. As they fly, Early can see lights inside a few windows, a yellow curtain, a patch of stained glass, pigeons asleep on sills, people shuffling along a sidewalk. Heads are tucked against the cold. One figure pulls a cart. *No place to go. Still moving, though,* whispers an unfamiliar voice. Early wonders if she is overhearing strangers' thoughts.

She knows they're heading home, as Dash said. And that the home they will land at will, oddly, have a brick-red roof and a broken chimney. An ember of worry glows inside her as she flies, worry that Dash won't make it. The moon shines huge and bright.

Dash had told her what to do. But what did *research rhythms* mean? *Re-search rhy-thms . . . re-search rhy-thms . . .*

Early jolted awake, feeling Sum's hand on her shoulder. "Did you see Dash?" Early asked. "We were flying!"

"Early, baby, you were having a bad dream." Sum was up on one elbow, her voice groggy.

"No, no! A good one. And I know what to do," Early whispered. Sum said nothing, but rubbed her daughter's back until her breathing leveled into sleep.

Crimp

The moment Early's eyes opened in the morning, she wrote down her dream. First she underlined *research rhythms* in black, counting the fifteen letters — 1 + 5 = 6, but then what?

As she washed her face, she ran the two words through her head, noticing the *re-rhy* sounds. She brushed her teeth, the syllables foaming along, and wondered if Dash also had sounds run through his head in a steady beat, an invisible rhythm that kept time with everyday life. She was pretty sure he did.

Mrs. Happadee walked them to school again, but without Aisha, who had a bad cold. Early missed walking next to her new friend; they might have talked about last night's amazing dream. Instead, Early said good morning to each of the people she passed on the street who were asking for money. She looked up at the cool, oyster-shell sky and smiled; she *knew* now what it felt like to fly. It was like you could be friends with the wind, which whistled in a silvery current along the side of your body. You could steer simply by rolling one way or the other.

She wondered if her dream was only from seeing *Peter Pan*. But *no*, Dash had visited them last night! He had shown her how to leave the shelter with Jubie and Sum, and how to *head home*, wherever that might be. He had spoken to her, and she knew that wasn't imagined. It felt as real as the buildings and people around her now. She walked into fifth grade that morning with her back straight, feeling almost like her old self.

The class was huge and noisy. The teacher, Ms. Chaff, a nervous young woman with a buzz cut and a little-kid voice, had barely noticed she had a new student this week. Early didn't mind. Less attention was a relief. Ms. Chaff's teaching seemed mostly about handing out work sheets, seeing the work done quietly, and collecting the results. So far, they'd studied a list of spelling words that all began with *dis* (*dissatisfied*, *dismay*, *dismiss*, *dismantle*), which caught Early's attention, as no other teacher she'd had ever selected words that way for a spelling lesson. Next came a map of the United States; each state had to be labeled and spelled correctly. Early got Rhode Island, Arkansas, Massachusetts, and Tennessee wrong.

At lunchtime she made herself a sandwich, took it over to the counter where you picked up forks and napkins, and slipped it into her backpack. Then she hurried back to the office.

"Mrs. B.'s in a meeting?" Early's face fell. "Did she leave any messages for Early Pearl? Or a phone number?" The person at the front desk shook his head.

Early sat down in the hallway and ate her lunch. She drank from the water fountain and went into the library.

Pulling out one of the fresh homemade notebooks, she printed *Word Book* on the cover.

First she looked up *research*, which had a French root. The work of a spy! Early smiled as she planted the word.

Next came *rhythm*, from Latin and Greek roots: any kind of movement with recurring strong and weak parts; an on-off beat, as of sound and silence; a harmonious pattern. Langston would add that rhythm could be found flowing from a pencil, tucked within a flower, or humming outward from almost any engine.

Could a gemstone have a rhythm?

Something was missing in what she understood. Early could *feel* it.

She glanced up to see a gray-haired figure with baggy clothes, wrinkled skin, and huge, red ears. Walking with a stiff-legged limp, he passed the library door.

The man at the front desk spoke with him. Then there was an announcement over the school loudspeaker: "Will Early Pearl please come to the office?"

Her heart pounding, afraid to believe this might be who she wanted it to be, Early put away her Word Book and stood as straight as she could.

"Help me, Dash," she said softly.

Crimp

The man took two awkward steps toward Early and shook her hand. His was bony and pale, still cool from being outside, and she knew hers was sweaty.

"Well, hello, Early Pearl!" he said, his voice a raspy whisper. Early forced herself to look up. The man was smiling and frowning at the same time, something Early came to learn was a tactic. You couldn't help but focus on someone who seemed both mad and glad.

"Hello, hello!" he growled, following that with a long, painful cough. "Pardon," he gasped. "Smoker's lungs."

"That's okay." Early smiled and blinked. "Thanks, Mr. Waive. Thanks for finding me!"

"Mind if we talk someplace?" Mr. Waive asked the man behind the desk. "I was her father's teacher, and her father was one superlative student. I got a call from a Mrs. B. who works in your office, and I want to hear the news."

Superlative, Early thought, as in *superman.*

"Sure, no problem. How about in this meeting room here?" It had a glass wall and a door that closed.

"Perfect," Mr. Waive and Early said in one voice, and this time Early got a relaxed smile from the older man, a smile that divided his face into parentheses of stubbly skin. His teeth, Early noticed, were a brownish yellow.

They sat. Early told.

Mr. Waive crossed his arms on his chest and looked down while she talked, as if he knew that was easier for her than having a strange grown-up look directly at her.

Early filled him in on their family and all that had happened since that terrible day in January, minus the diamond news. She ended with the warrant out for Dash's arrest.

There was a moment of silence. Early looked at her lap and then back at Mr. Waive. Was he going to get up and leave?

He uncrossed his arms and rubbed his eyes roughly with both palms, so hard that the skin took a moment to settle back into place. Pressing his hands flat on the table, he looked directly at Early. "You are Dashel's daughter, that's clear."

Early nodded. "He said that to me a lot." As she looked back at Mr. Waive, she noticed with a flash of fright that he had a dark mole on one eyelid, just as the man with the mask had. The man who had lifted her up and said scary things. *That is a silly coincidence,* she said to herself quickly. *Silly.*

"That means," Mr. Waive was saying, "you will understand what I have to tell you. Dreams matter, but they aren't always to be shared."

Early was startled. He *couldn't* know about her dream last night. She nodded again. Now he was doing the mad-glad expression.

"I mean," Mr. Waive rasped on, "that your father may have shared more dreams than was wise at that library. It's a public place. A big place. Anyone can enter, and anyone can listen. He was — I mean, is, *IS*! — a brilliant young man, one with such a good mind that it must have been noticed, possibly for the wrong reasons. The question is, by whom."

Suddenly Mr. Waive was on his feet and pacing, taking uneven steps, first one way and then the other. He moved amazingly well for such an unhealthy-looking man, and one with a serious limp. Early thought of the *Treasure Island* pirate with one leg.

"Coercion," he muttered. "Some form of coercion."

Early wasn't sure if he was talking to her. What did the word mean?

"History and Social Sciences . . ." Mr. Waive stopped abruptly. "That's where. But why? Why did he trust them?" Early didn't know what to say, or even if Mr. Waive was talking to her. She shrugged, a small movement just to let him know she was listening.

"Probably for predictable reasons: the thrill of unauthorized complicity and an opportunity to glean, using intelligence. Participation is a given, but we'll have to be circumspect," Mr. Waive was now saying. "It's obvious that your father stepped into something even he, with his faceted outlook, didn't read correctly. Or perhaps he simply didn't see it; a key element was hidden. A deliberate crimp that covered a clue." A shower of words to plant in the Word Book! Early then realized what he'd said. *Participation.*

"Can I come to the library?" she asked.

He answered by not answering, saying only, "One step ahead. I knew it."

Early was beginning to understand what Dash had said about Mr. Waive; he scattered the pieces but didn't look back to see what you did with them, as if he knew you'd figure things out. She saw how her father, as a boy, might never have forgotten.

What she didn't exactly see was how Mr. Waive could be so willing, so quickly, to help her now. She knew Dash was special, but something about all this felt too easy. Too fast.

Sum would sort it out, she told herself. "You'll have to meet my mother," she said.

Mr. Waive nodded, as if Early had been making small talk about the weather. "The sum of the parts," he muttered to himself. "Quite brilliant."

Early felt almost dizzy, but suddenly lighter. Again, a bubble of hope was rising inside her.

"Can you come to the shelter?" Early asked, then wished she hadn't. After all, he'd just come to the school to find her, and only a day after she'd left a message. "If you have time," she added.

"Real time I don't have, but time for you, I do," he said. "I'll be there after dinner tonight."

"We eat at —" Early began.

"Oh, I know," Mr. Waive said. "Never forget." He turned, left the room, and lurched down the hall at an amazing speed.

Early sat for a moment in the conference area, wondering how to think about what had just happened. She opened her Word Book and wrote down *coershun, complicity, circumspect, glean, faceted, crimp.* Some were familiar, some not, but these were the six he'd emphasized. The bell rang, and she couldn't get back to the dictionary.

The rest of the day dragged. When she happened to look at the clock and it was 2:22, she smiled. "Okay, Dash," she whispered. Without her father near, those last number entries in his notebook felt like a message. Whenever she noticed a pattern that he'd seen, too, she felt as if he knew it, like he'd left her a clue.

Crimp

Mr. Waive was a different man around Sum.

He spoke more slowly. He'd shaved and even combed his hair. It was as if he knew he had to behave more normally. Early watched and wondered.

"I retired early because of bad health: lung disease and rotten knees. Then my sister and her kids needed a place to live. Her husband died, and she had no income. It was like a game of dominoes. One piece fell, knocking down another."

Sum nodded. "So sorry," she murmured.

"My pension is stretched to the breaking point," he whispered in that gravelly voice, "otherwise I'd try to help you more directly. But what I *can* do is some undercover investigating at the library. I'll pretend to do research in Dashel's department, and ask some questions. Observe. Poke around."

"That would be wonderful!" Sum brightened immediately. "I've been dying to go in again myself, but of course I can't — I'm instantly recognizable. And let me tell you, it's a waking nightmare to feel so powerless. Invisible, yet *too* visible, if you know what I mean."

Mr. Waive nodded, then shook his head, as if drawing tic-tac-toe boards in the air. He left without asking Sum if Early could come. Perhaps it was because Jubie had whined, "Can I go? Got lollipops there!" and Sum had said quickly, "Not this time, son."

Early had to admit she was relieved.

Mr. Skip Waive was overwhelming one-on-one, and she wasn't sure she was smart enough to keep up with him. *Dash, who is this person?* she asked silently. When there was no response, she looked again at the new list of words. Why did Mr. Waive use such strange vocabulary around an eleven-year-old?

And why, it suddenly occurred to her, hadn't Dash tried to find him in recent years, especially since this teacher had helped a boy without parents believe he could succeed in the world? A boy who became a generous, outgoing man?

As Dash had taught her to do, she tried spinning Mr. Waive around in her imagination, but all she could see was that black mole on his eyelid and his way of grinning and frowning at the same time.

It was odd for a retired teacher with hardly any voice, but he felt like someone with deep secrets. And secrets, in Early's world, were almost always dangerous.

Crimp

At lunchtime on Monday, Early was alone again. Gulping down a sandwich in the hall, she hurried back into the library. Aisha was still out sick. Making friends at this new school, after her experience with Slippery Braid and the other girls in the cafeteria, was no longer a part of the plan.

She pulled out the Word Book and got to work on Mr. Waive's list of six. The first three — *coercion* (tough spelling!), *complicity*, and *circumspect* — were about being forced to agree, or being dominated; about working with someone else on something that wasn't right; about being cautious, thinking of the consequences. Early didn't much like this pile of *C* words. It was too much of a wrong-right tangle.

The second three were easier. *Glean* meant something her family was already good at: gathering what's been left behind, or picking up relevant information. *Glean* gleamed, gentle and smooth. *Faceted* was what a cut gemstone was, and what made a diamond sparkle in bright light. *Crimp* she knew, as Dash had added it to their onomatopoeia list.

While working her way halfheartedly through math problems that afternoon, she rolled the words around and around, ending up with *glean*, *coercion*, *faceted*, *complicity*, *crimp*, *circumspect.*

In that order, they told a story that might explain what had happened to Dash. Her heart sank, and she knew Sum was right: Mr. Waive was, at the moment, their best and only hope. Dash was caught in something complicated, a mess with too many meanings for Early to sort out on her own.

Crack, *from the Middle English* crakken

Verb: to break, split, or snap with a sharp sound; to fall apart under pressure; to solve a mystery, decipher a code, or understand a problem after much thought; to strike; to break through a barrier; to open a book, as for studying.

Noun: a loud noise; a narrow opening; a joke; a break in a surface; an opportunity.

Crack

Another day went by, and no Mr. Waive.

Early's time in school circled around checking the office for a message or a missed visit. She half-expected Mr. Waive to show up outside the door one day at dismissal and whiz her off to the Harold Washington Library. Just in case, she kept a note from Sum in her pocket.

It never happened. Early pulled out the note and looked at it so many times that the edges became worn. She felt guilty now that she'd ever thought Mr. Waive was scary; she hoped they hadn't frightened him away.

Aisha had pneumonia. She'd been rushed to the hospital one night and the next day her mom had left the shelter. Mrs. Happadee promised to let Early know as soon as she heard where Aisha and her mom had gone. Early felt sad she hadn't had a chance to say good-bye, and already missed her one good friend.

Sum visited a day care center with Jubie that week. The only place with an opening was in a dank basement with dirty floors, a TV blaring in the corner, a broken bathroom sink, and just a few blocks and dolls. Most of the kids were crying on the day Sum and Jubie walked in.

Each afternoon when Early got back from school, she went straight upstairs to find Jubie. Her brother was growing more and more difficult and restless. He whined lots, and had a constant cough and runny nose. Sum seemed barely to notice. When Early took him, it at least gave Sum a chunk of time to make calls. If the tutoring room wasn't open, Early played with Jubie until dinner.

She'd found a box of half-broken crayons in the trash at school, and squirreled away paper from the recycling bin outside her classroom. Now her brother could do some coloring. She tried to explain that he shouldn't use all the paper at once but that only made him cry, so she watched sadly as he filled a handful of sheets with bold blue and yellow scribbles in about ten minutes.

Sum had seemed to perk up after Mr. Waive's visit, but as each day passed with no word from Dash's old teacher, Early watched her mother slip further and further down some kind of crack. One afternoon when Early went upstairs to find Jubie, Sum was simply lying on the lower bunk in their fort, her eyes barely open, while Jubie used his toothbrush to shoot everyone who walked by. "Pow! You're dead! No more talking!" he said, over and over. When Early took Jubie downstairs and told Sum, "Okay, there's still time for calls today," her mother didn't move or even answer. Early saw Mrs. Happadee a few minutes later and said, "My mother isn't doing too well. Can you help her find an okay place to take Jubie so she can get going on a job?"

Mrs. Happadee sighed. "I've given her all the references I have. Maybe I can move you-all to your own room one of these days. Then maybe she'll feel a little more like herself." She patted Early on the back. "Your mom is lucky to have you," she said.

Jubie, meanwhile, had started pulling on Early. "Don't want

to go no place! Want to stay with you and Sum!" he moaned, half-crying as he pulled on her hand. Then a coughing fit started, disgusting stuff poured down his face, and Early had to hurry him to a bathroom to get him cleaned up.

Many of the kids in the shelter were sick with an endless round of colds. Of the group she'd met that first day in the tutoring room, only one or two had returned, and Early began to understand that was the way things went at Helping Hand: Families dropped out of programs, suffered through emergencies, had to move overnight. No one seemed surprised when a kid stayed out of school or didn't come to meals; no one asked where he or she was, as if missing stuff was just part of life.

Early decided she couldn't wait another day for Mr. Waive. Tomorrow she'd ask in the office at school for his number and then she'd call him herself. Maybe he didn't realize how bad things were, or how desperately they needed to find Dash.

He couldn't see that Sum and Jubie were both falling apart and that no one but Early seemed to know it.

Crack

At bedtime that night Early asked Sum to read more *Treasure Island*. She shook her head. "Just don't have the heart, baby. I'm sorry, I really am," she murmured. "Plus, it's a little too close to what's real. Too painful to read right now."

Early said, her voice getting louder and louder, "But you've *got* to have the heart, Sum! And we don't have *pirates* here! You gotta read and you can't give up! Jubie and I need you so badly, and Dash needs you even more. What about rescuing Dash? You're the grown-up, and you can't give up! What about Dashsumearlyjubie? What would Dash say if he saw you like this?"

Sum's face crumpled and her voice got high and squeaky. "He'd say, 'What's *wrong* with you, baby? We got places to go and things to do!' It's just — it's just — so hard. I can't see a way out of this, you know? I'm losing hope. Maybe Dash isn't coming back." The tears were running freely down Sum's face now.

Early yelled at her mother, "*Stop it!* You can't talk that way!" and ran downstairs. She heard Jubie crying at the top of the stairs, calling, "Early! Don't go away! Don't be mad! Keep me caaaam-pany!"

Early sat down at one of the eating tables, put her head in her arms, and tried to hide her tears. Soon someone was rubbing her back. Early looked up to see Velma, the woman who had first spoken to them when they'd gotten to Helping Hand, who'd lost her kids and many of her teeth.

"I heard you up there. Your mama's a good one, now. She's a good one. Maybe it's up to you. Sometimes kids can do a better job than their parents when life gets mean. We try, but we got confusions."

These words comforted Early. She looked at Velma. "Yeah," she said. "Thanks."

"You go on back and tell her you love her. That's all a mama needs to hear."

"Yeah," Early said, realizing Velma probably never got to hear that from her kids.

Things could be worse; they were still three. Early walked slowly back up the stairs, splashed her face with cold water, and headed over to their cluster.

Sum was up and opening drawers with a jerk, one after the other, moving faster and faster. "Hey, where is it? Where's our *First Book of Rhythms*? I was going to read a few pages aloud to you two tonight, just to bring us back to happier times, but I don't see it. Early, did you take it to school?"

Early shook her head. "Of course not. And I'm sorry, Sum. I didn't mean —"

"Jubie!" Sum shouted, her voice strange and shrill. "You didn't do anything with it, did you?"

Jubie's eyes got big, and he whispered, "I gave it to a boy. He let me play with his truck."

"Which boy? Which?" Sum was crouched in front of Jubie now, and her intensity frightened both kids.

"It's okay, Sum, I'll look around," Early said, and began to walk between the bunks, asking for the book. "Seen our old family read-aloud? My brother gave it to a boy in this room, and we're sorry but we want it back. Anyone got it?"

Sum rushed around the room after Early, shouting at everyone. Jubie couldn't seem to remember which boy he'd given it to. No one offered to give it back. The guard came over and threatened to call Mrs. Happadee if Sum didn't simmer down.

Sum then turned her back on Jubie, who was now wailing; Early had to step in and quiet him down. When he finally fell asleep, she lay awake, feeling angry, but this time not at Sum. Her mother was obviously in trouble. How dare someone keep their book, a book Dash had found for the family, when they'd asked for it back? She peeked out at the tiny slivers of light coming through the shelter blinds, and thought about what it felt like to fly. To escape.

Crack

Before going to school the next morning, Early printed big signs and put them all over the shelter:

Missing! The First Book of Rhythms. Means lots to the Pearl family. Please return if you have it. We thank you.

When she got to school, she went directly into the office. Mrs. B. was there and beamed a cheery hello. "Well, you're the girl with the pearl, aren't you! The girl with the pretty name."

Early nodded and tried to look pleasant; her smile felt stiff.

"I'm wondering if you could give me Mr. Waive's phone

number." Early paused, and Mrs. B. blinked. Early hurried on, "I have something new to tell him. He came here last week to meet me, when you were out of the office, and then he even came to our shelter that night and talked with my mom and little brother." She stopped for breath. "Please," she added.

Mrs. B.'s nails, pink this time, strolled across the counter while she looked at the ceiling. "Well, if he didn't give it to you himself, I'm sorry, honey. I can't do that. No wiggle room in rules."

"Ohhh." Early looked so sad that Mrs. B. said, "But I *could* leave something on the counter by mistake."

"Oh!" Early said. "Yes, maybe I'll stop back in at lunchtime. Wow, Mrs. B.!"

"Just a scrap of paper, no idea what's on it," she said cheerfully, and winked at Early.

That morning the classroom felt less strange. From her desk, Early looked around. Ms. Chaff smiled at her. "Why, you look so awake this morning! I'm trying to decide on a project for our first free-writing time this month. How about a recent dream you've had? How does that sound, kids?"

Early scowled, and Ms. Chaff paused, confused. "Or any dream you remember and would like to share with us," she added.

Some of the boys snickered and there was a creaking of chairs. Ms. Chaff looked irritated. "Look. Okay. Write about what you'd like to, but it needs to be appropriate. A wish or a dream. You may have to read it aloud."

Early wondered what on earth she could say. She couldn't talk about Dash visiting them and teaching her to fly, or Velma, who'd lost her kids, or her upset little brother and sad mother, both of whom cried all the time now. Or Dash, who was the best and smartest father in the world and was wanted by the police. But she could . . .

She bent over, scribbling madly. As she wrote, her face relaxed and a tiny smile appeared.

In what seemed like no time, but was really twenty minutes, Ms. Chaff interrupted with, "Okay, that's all we can do today. Early, would you read yours to us?"

Early froze, suddenly remembering the girl with the braids in the lunchroom. Was it safe to read what she'd written? The room was quiet. She shook her head.

"Oh, come on!" Ms. Chaff had her hands on her hips and was pleading in an embarrassing way now.

"Well, okay," Early agreed, feeling as though any more of a fuss would make things worse. "This is about a house in our old neighborhood, and my family and I had a kind of dream about it. We used our imaginations."

"Very *good*," Ms. Chaff said encouragingly.

Her stomach churning, Early read:

"*What if you could pick where you lived? What if you could pick a house and make it just like you wanted? My family and I used to play that game, especially with a home we walked by in Woodlawn.*

"It always had a cat in the front window and red roses in the yard every summer. There was a swing on the porch and rocking chairs. If I lived in

that house, I'd change the curtains from white to lace so lots of light came in. I'd hang a crystal in my bedroom window so that rainbows danced around the walls. I'd make a big sign that said Welcome to the Pearl Home *right next to the doorbell."*

Early paused, swallowing. Something about the words *Pearl Home* sounded so far away, like they came from someone else's story. She went on:

"My little brother said he'd drive his trucks on the walk all day and eat cookies on the front steps. My dad would mow the lawn and paint the kitchen a sky blue. He loves to read and wants bookshelves in every room. My mom would sit on the porch, be happy again, and watch everyone go by. And at Christmas we'd have a tree with a thousand lights and balls and ornaments, sparkling away in the living room. When you looked in from outside, you'd think, That is my dream home!"

She shuffled her two pages together in a neat pile, and sat absolutely still.

Ms. Chaff dabbed her nose with a tissue and said, "That is so moving. Just beautiful, Early!"

From the back of the room, someone mimicked, "*Just* beautiful," and sniffed loudly.

Ms. Chaff spun around. "Who said that? Jason? I'd like you to read yours now."

There was a scuffling, shuffling sound and then a slow voice began:

"I dream about having money so we don't have to worry anymore. So we can get me a stunt bike and get my teenage sister a big TV, so her friends will want to come over. So we can hang some things on the windows and

walls of our home. It's always so bare and we don't got no decorations. My dad sits on the couch all day and wants a job. My mom comes home from work and yells at him 'cause there's toys everywhere and beer bottles tipped over and dishes in the sink. Money is always in my dreams."

Ms. Chaff said, "Ver-ry good. My. Home is a big thing, isn't it?"

Silence. "Not really," a girl said, and giggled. "Kind of bo-ring." There was tittering.

Early suddenly felt a spurt of fury. She turned around in her chair to face the girl who'd spoken and the other kids who were smiling. "That's the dumbest thing I ever heard! Try life *without* a home and you won't laugh about it. Try not having even one family bedroom or even one parent with a job. Try sleeping with a ton of other strangers in the same room. Try having your dad vanish and having a mom who used to be happy and is now sad or mad all the time. Try waiting in line to eat every meal and waiting in line to make a phone call. Just TRY it!" Early jumped out of her seat and ran, bumping into three or four desks on the way.

Once out in the hall, she bolted blindly toward the bathroom, locked herself into a stall, and sobbed. What had she *done*? Now she'd *never* be able to face anyone in this school again! She dried the tears on her sleeve and sat quietly, trying to figure out what to do next. The bell rang.

Soon the bathroom filled up with girls, and to her horror, kids kept rattling the handle on her stall. "Hurry *up*! I gotta *go*! Who's in there?"

Early covered her mouth and said, "I'll be right out," hoping that would disguise her voice. Then she heard, "Ohhh, it's the *homeless* girl! The one who read in class!" followed by "Shhhh, that's not nice," and then, "Whoever you are, you're not early any longer, you're gonna be late if you don't get goin'!" and then, "Can't make a home in a toilet, won't work," followed by a wave of laughter.

Early flung open the door. "*Who* said that?"

Her voice shook but she felt strong with anger. No one answered. "Whoever you are, *you* are the worst person I've ever met! I hope you lose your home and — and — everyone in your family leaves you behind and you have to start begging for food!" Early slammed her shoulder into the metal door of the stall, making one of the girls stagger backward. Elbowing her way past the others, she stomped on a bunch of sneakers.

A chorus of "Oooh, she hurt me!" and "Ow, I'm tellin'!" drifted out of the bathroom behind her.

She was dying to leave school and go back to the shelter on her own, but knew the guard at the exit would stop her. Glancing toward the door, Early almost missed what she then absorbed: The chair, miraculously, was empty. Not a soul to be seen. Maybe only for seconds! She ran as fast as she could and burst outside into the cold, bright air.

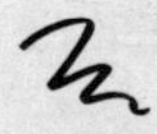

Crack

Pulling up the hood on her sweatshirt, Early walked as fast as she could, slipping and sliding on the icy sidewalk.

She passed a group of police officers and glanced nervously in their direction, but they had bigger problems. One prodded a person wrapped in about a hundred jackets, a lump lying against a building. No face was visible, but the head shook no again and again. Early felt like telling the police to leave the poor soul alone, but she kept going.

Another cop bent over a form slumped in the doorway of a boarded-up building. "No response," he called out, to someone sitting in a patrol car at the curb.

Early shuddered and hurried on. Even a week ago she would've been shocked at the thought of someone dying outside in this neighborhood, but not anymore.

She knew shelter rules were that no kids were allowed in unless their parent was there also. *Sum, you better be here, oh, please!* she prayed over and over as she hurried down the block.

Grabbing the shelter door, she yanked it open and bumped right into Mrs. Happadee. "Oh, my, Early! You've got everyone so worried. The school just called. What happened?"

Early felt her legs wobble beneath her and she plopped down onto a carton of plastic forks that had just been unloaded by a food supply truck. "I want my mother," she moaned. "Can you get my mother?"

Mrs. Happadee frowned. "Your mother just took your little brother to the hospital, his cough was so bad."

"Ohhh . . ." Early's breath whooshed out in a long, shaky sigh. "Please don't make me go back to the school!" she pleaded.

Mrs. Happadee put her arm around Early and walked her into the office. She sat her down in the corner and shut the glass door. Returning to the front desk, the shelter director made a couple of phone calls.

Soon a policewoman walked in the door. Early felt her heart drop through the floor and zoom into outer space. Was she being *arrested*?

The policewoman walked toward her, as if in slow motion, with Mrs. Happadee now beside her. Early froze.

The door opened and Mrs. Happadee said, "Early, this officer is going to take you to the hospital to be with your mother and brother. And I'll walk you upstairs to get a change of clothes and all three of your toothbrushes, just in case you folks are there for the night."

Early nodded, unable to speak. They walked up the stairs. When they got to the Pearl cluster, there, on the floor between the bunks, was *The First Book of Rhythms*. Early pounced on it and gave it a hug. The paper jacket was a bit more ragged and the green cover beneath had a new streak of dirt, but it looked as though it was still in one piece.

"Thanks," she breathed to Mrs. Happadee as they headed downstairs. She tucked the book into a plastic bag with their supplies.

"Here, this is clean," Mrs. Happadee said, handing Early a long, mud-brown parka. "I always keep an emergency supply, especially when we get such a cold winter."

Early slipped her arms into the jacket. It covered her hands. "Thanks so much, Mrs. Happadee," she said. "I didn't mean to leave my stuff at school."

"I know, dear, and I'll find it when I go in to pick up the kids this afternoon."

Early rode alone in the back of the patrol car, imagining that this was what it might feel like to be Dash if the police found him before his family did.

They sped by the entrance to the school. Early ducked down and pretended to tie her sneaker, just in case one of the kids spotted her through a window. Not that she was ever going back there. Just in case.

Her whole life felt like a bunch of just-in-case moments now. Eating in the school hallway, just in case someone made her feel bad again; checking the recycling a bunch of times, just in case there was almost-unused paper for Jubie; rushing upstairs as soon as she was back from school, just in case Sum needed the time before dinner for phone calls.

And now oh, *no*! Early realized with a surge of frustration that Mrs. B. had left Mr. Waive's telephone number for her to "find" at lunchtime, just in case she truly needed it. She did! But now she'd be labeled as the Difficult Homeless Girl if she went back, and Mrs. B. would never dare to do that again.

The city spinning by outside the windows of the patrol car looked bleak and unkind, a landscape of doors and windows that said, *never, never, never.*

Crack

When Early peeked through the curtains in the hospital emergency room, Sum shrieked and almost crushed her with a surprised hug. Early threw her arms around her mother's neck, something she hadn't done in ages. Jubie grinned and made excited snorting sounds from behind his oxygen mask. Sum explained that he'd had a coughing fit that morning and then couldn't seem to catch his breath. The doctors diagnosed pneumonia with a sinus infection, and had already started him on antibiotics. They assured Sum that he'd be feeling like his usual, bouncy self in no time.

Early pulled *Rhythms* out of her bag, and both Sum and Jubie clapped as if she'd done a magic trick. The hospital was welcoming, feeding them all a lunch of grilled cheese and grapes. They felt almost giddy. For the first time since they'd gotten to the shelter, the three Pearls were on their own, out of the cold and in a brightly lit place where they could talk freely.

Early spilled the story of the whole rotten morning, including the missed opportunity to get Mr. Waive's number.

Sum listened intently, then said, "We gotta get ourselves moving somehow. That shelter is a godsend, of course, but there're enough germs to bring down an army, and it's so *hard* to get anything done! Here's an idea, Early: Why don't we homeschool you for a bit? Then I can actually go and apply for some jobs, leaving you and Jubie together in a lobby or a store for a few minutes; we can visit libraries, go to free places in the city, and *think* again. I feel like I can't get my head together when we're there, night and day; it's like living inside a subway station, so busy and noisy all the time. And even when you make a phone call, people can hear what you're saying. There's just no privacy, ever!"

Early brightened at the thought of homeschooling, but then paused. "How can I do anything but take care of Jubie, though, if you're working? And you know we can't stay in the shelter alone."

"Mmm," Sum said. "Well, let's take it a step at a time. As Dash says, we got it all, meaning we're young and strong and we have each other. Just gotta make it work. Let's start, when we get out of the hospital today, by checking every want ad in the papers. Look, I picked up free copies in the lobby here. Might find some wonderful old grandma to watch Jubie when he gets better and I'm working! And by then we will have sorted out the whole school mess. We'll do fine, with or without that Mr. Waive."

Early felt almost happy as the three returned to the shelter that night. She listened to her mom telling Mrs. Happadee that Jubie was now on medicine and already feeling better, and that Early would be studying on her own for a bit. Mrs. Happadee brought them the missing coat and backpack, which she'd rescued from a locker at school, but looked concerned at the news about not returning to Hughes.

"Ever homeschooled before, Mrs. Pearl?" she asked.

"Well, no, but Early has always been ahead and loves to read."

"I'm sure she's a wonderful student, but life at a shelter is a big adjustment already, as you know, and we don't want her to fall behind her grade level. There's math and science to study. . . ."

"No worries, Mrs. Happadee. She won't be out long," Sum said. Early nodded, not knowing if this was the truth.

When they were upstairs and tucked into bed, Sum read aloud the first chapter from *Rhythms*, and Langston's company felt perfect.

Early loved the grace with which he described drawing circles, one inside the other:

See how these circles almost seem to move, for you have left something of your own movement there, and your own feeling of place and of roundness. Your circles are not quite like the circles of anyone else in the world, because you are not like anyone else.

When a Jubie-sized face peeked through the curtains around their cluster and asked, "You got your book?" Sum smiled. As soon as she did, the boy muttered, "It was me who had it, but I was scared to give it back yesterday, you was so mad." Then he added in a whisper, "And my mama woulda whupt me if she'd knowed."

Sum patted his hand and said, "I won't tell. And besides, you didn't do anything wrong — Jubie gave it to you! I was just upset and homesick. This is a family book and it means a whole lot to us. I'll be sure my son returns your truck tomorrow. And hey, want to listen?"

The boy shrugged, grinned, and curled against Jubie, who was now fast asleep. He listened to a couple of pages before sleeping, too, and when his mother came to scoop him up off the bunk, she thanked Sum for reading. She explained that she couldn't see well enough to read aloud to her kids, but both Early and Sum knew the truth was something else: This mother could barely read. They'd seen her struggling with a newsletter from the school. At least Sum had finished high school and had the advantage of all those years of sharing books with Dash.

"You're lucky, Sum," Early said.

Understanding what she meant, Sum sighed. "I guess I am. Reading is a tool no one can take away. A million bad things may happen in life and it'll still be with you, like a flashlight that never needs a battery. Reading can offer a crack of light on the blackest of nights."

Early looked carefully at her mother's face. "You sound like Dash now."

"Do I?" Sum smiled with her eyes, one of the saddest smiles Early had ever seen.

Chase, *from the Anglo-French* chacer

Verb: to rush after, follow or pursue in order to catch.

Noun: an event in which living creatures are hunted.

Chase, *from the Anglo-French* enchaser

Verb: to decorate metal by indenting with a delicate hammer and tools, sometimes adding gems.

Chase, *from the Middle French* chasse *and Latin* capsa

Noun: a rectangular metal frame used for printing.

Chase

Up, down, up, down: Early felt like life was starting to copy the line patterns at the beginning of *The First Book of Rhythms.* Some days there was hope, and a landscape in sight; other days it felt like her family had fallen down and would never get up again. If there was a rhythm here, it sure didn't feel easy.

The Chicago Public Library had always been a source of great pride for the Pearls. Dash was thrilled by his connection to the Harold Washington branch, and felt as though he belonged there. Sum and the kids loved the second-floor Children's Library, which was huge and always packed with new titles. Inside this building, the world had felt generous, limitless, like a safe spot for dreams to grow.

The largest public library facility in the world, the place is a brick and rose-colored granite fortress with soaring windows, an elegant conversation between stone and glass. Perched at each corner of the roof, massive green metal owls peer out from leafy plants. Early had thought they were storybook creatures meant to welcome kids until Dash had explained that owls symbolize knowledge and wisdom.

Rhythms are a fact on the outside of this building: Horizontal bands encircling each story are crossed by a vertical design of cornstalks cascading downward at intervals. Layers of rounded framing echo windows and soften the geometry of the whole. At street level, many doors open on each side. It is a castle that welcomes.

Named after former mayor Harold Washington, a can-do man who was Chicago's first African American to run the city, the structure whispers, *Yes! Whoever you are, come in! This building is for you!* It is so large that it has its own stop on the elevated train. Everyone is invited in, no matter what age or stage, and all nationalities are welcome. Early remembered Dash explaining to her that people without homes often came to get warm in the winter or cool in the summer, and that the library was a kind place, even to those who were too unwell or tired to read. A refuge, he called it.

Early opened her eyes one morning and suddenly *knew* that this was where she should be each day. And maybe, just maybe, she'd discover where Dash had gone. It was a place that had been the center of their lives. If something had gone wrong for Dash, it could only be because of a tangle. A tangle! And, of course, tangles didn't fix themselves. Early couldn't wait to get to work. Kids had small fingers, and small fingers were good at knots.

When she asked Sum at breakfast if the three of them could go, Early didn't mention to her mother that she was planning to return to the library every day, each and every day, until she figured out what was going on. Sum thought this was just an expedition, and Early knew better than to say any more.

The train stop near the shelter was close, only three blocks away, and it took you right to Harold Washington. Early watched carefully, memorizing the route and the number of stops. The elevated train, a hundred-year-old system that creaked and trembled, snaked through a few different neighborhoods on its way downtown. Early got a glimpse of boarded-up houses and apartment buildings. She'd seen places like these in Woodlawn, but they'd never meant anything. Now, quite suddenly, they did.

Every window and door was covered with plywood, and sometimes there was a huge padlock on the entrance. Surrounding these buildings was trash, and lots of it: parts of cars, old tires, sinks and toilets, broken furniture, sometimes bags of clothing scattered through weeds. Here and there you might see an old lawn chair still standing or a one-handled tricycle. Some buildings bore the smoky scars of fires and jagged holes in the roofs, but others looked fine. Just empty. These places were sad, the word *home* still echoing around the brick and wood. *Home.* Early thought about how it must hurt to look at a place where you used to live and see it so neglected, as if you were long gone. Like the building had died, and its eyes and mouth were closed, nailed shut. It was a spooky thought.

"Sum," she said.

"Uh-uh," her mother replied. She was looking out the window, too.

"How come there are so many homes standing empty in Chicago and so many people like us who don't have a home? How come those empty homes aren't being fixed up and filled with people who need a place to live?"

"That is an A-number-one question, Early. I don't know the answer. It feels wrong and pretty crazy, doesn't it? Wasteful. Seems like it wouldn't take that much to make some of these places livable again."

Early nodded. The three were quiet, watching the landscape of buildings roll by outside the train. The difference between a window with a glimpse of everyday life inside and a window with nothing but boards was startling.

She pushed her hood back and scratched one ear. "Hey! If some rich person, like a basketball player or a movie star, just adopted one home at a time and made it nice again for people to live in, but only people who couldn't afford a place, that would be so amazing. Folks could get on their feet, you know? Have an address! Hold a job!"

"I think it's brilliant, Early. You should write a bunch of letters to the people who run the city . . . and some millionaires. You might start something big."

"Someone else must have thought of that before, but you never know, Sum. Dash would say it was a great idea, wouldn't he?"

"He would," Sum said, her voice suddenly quieter. "He would."

"Maybe you can get us a house, Early," Jubie piped up. "A house with a yard. Can you? Then when Dash gets home, I'll be sitting on the steps waiting and he'll be sooooo surprised!"

"Yeah," Early said, "I'll try." She felt bad she'd gotten Jubie thinking about it. Sum said nothing for the rest of the ride.

Chase

Mrs. Wormser hurried from behind her desk. "Early! Early, Early, Early!"

After two giant hugs and a kiss in between, the librarian pulled back and said simply, "I don't believe it. Any of this. Just horrible."

Early explained her plan to Mrs. Wormser.

"Smart," the librarian agreed. "Go for it. You *may* uncover something, truly, but be careful. I'm not sure what's up around here, but none of us feel at ease with Mr. Pincer or that assistant he's brought in, Ms. Whissel. Have you met either of them?"

Early shook her head.

"You'll see what I mean. Now I'm off to the bathroom, and you just slip past my desk while I'm gone."

"Thanks." Early gave her a quick grin. "For everything. Oh, and Sum says hi. She and Jubie are downstairs in the Children's Library."

After checking the name tag and knocking softly on his open door, Early peeked around the corner. "Good morning, Mr. Pincer," she said, in a cheerful voice that she hoped sounded like a breath of fresh air. "Nice to meet you! I'm Early Pearl. Dashel's daughter." She'd known just where to go; Dash had often taken her into the Staff Only offices.

Mr. Pincer started to get up from his desk, sat down again, banged his knee, and then spilled his coffee. He popped the cup upright, mopped at the dark puddle with a handful of napkins from the doughnut shop down the street, and tried to smile.

"Welcome, welcome! Gotta say you surprised me!"

"I'm kind of surprising myself," Early said. "But here's what I want to do: Collect everyone's memories about my father. I can't really help the police figure out the whole mess; I know I'm just a kid, but Dash and I were superclose, and —"

Early broke off and looked down, waiting for Mr. Pincer to reach out. He did. "Of course, of course!" he said. "That's a marvelous idea. Of course you want to preserve memories. I'll do everything I can to help. Yes, to help," he repeated, as if he needed to hear himself say it again.

"That's great of you, Mr. Pincer," Early gushed. "I knew you'd understand. Do you have kids of your own?"

The man grunted, cleared his throat, and said, "No, no children. Not that lucky, I guess," he finished, with a pasted-on smile. "I guess," he added. Early wondered if he always repeated himself, or just didn't like kids.

She looked back down at her hands and said, "So, how would you like me to start? I'm not in school at the moment — I'm helping my mother and getting, well, adjusted. We're living in a shelter far away from our old neighborhood of Woodlawn, and Sum is looking for a job, but she hasn't found a place to leave Jubie yet. Everything in the shelter neighborhood is so, well, you know, *dangerous*. Dirty. And my brother, Jubie, got real sick with all the germs; he had to go to the hospital for oxygen, but he's coughing less now." Early paused for a gulp of air and looked up.

Mr. Pincer's pale brown eyes were looking paler. "A shelter, did you say? A shelter?"

"Yes, sir," Early said. Using *ma'am* or *sir* always gave a kid some kind of advantage.

"Oh, my. Yes, well. Well. Got food and warm enough?"

"They gave us blankets and sheets and toothbrushes, and Sum and Jubie and I all sleep in a bunk bed in a big room with a lot of other moms and kids. You wait in lines to get a meal and you wait in lines for everything, now that I think about it. After our apartment got destroyed —"

Mr. Pincer was leaning farther and farther back in his chair, as if that were the only escape option available. "*Destroyed?* Did you say *destroyed*? What happened? You'd better tell me, yes, tell me," he said, not sounding like he wanted to hear at all.

Early was feeling like things were going just right. "Oh, I thought you knew! Well, three men and a woman turned up in our apartment on the same day my mother came to see you here. Later on. At bedtime. They said they were police, then when Sum didn't open the door, they knocked it down. Scared us to death. They wanted something; they wrecked everything and left with all of our books and even our family notebooks. They took it all."

"All your books . . . All, all . . ." Mr. Pincer echoed faintly. He picked up one of the coffee-soaked paper napkins and dabbed at his forehead, leaving a wet smear peppered with grounds and sugar.

"And then," Early continued breathlessly, "Sum was sheltering us kids with her body, and it was awful, we were all crying, and one of the men pushed Sum and she hit her head. Big bruise. Then he tried to pull me away, but Sum grabbed me back."

"Oh, my," Mr. Pincer was muttering. "Oh, my. I wonder why — I mean who — did your mother tell the police?"

"Of course."

"And . . . do you know what the four people wanted?" Mr. Pincer asked, leaning forward slightly in his chair. "Do you know?"

"No, sir," Early said promptly. "Do you?"

"Ha, well, huff!" The chair snapped backward. "Of course not, not, not!" Mr. Pincer looked like it was hard work pulling himself off the *nots*.

"It *is* a knot, isn't it? I mean, a tangle." Early couldn't resist this one.

Mr. Pincer looked sharply at her for the first time. "Your father used to enjoy wordplay as well, yes, just as well, I mean —" He broke off and rubbed his hand over his forehead, then looked at it as if it had betrayed him. He wiped the nastiness off on his pants.

"It's a very strange thing, you see, as if it all had nothing to do with Dash at all. At all," Early added, just to make Mr. Pincer feel at home with the repeating. She paused, then whispered, "You heard, of course, about the diamond."

"Diamond!" Mr. Pincer's hand now shot up onto the desk. It opened and closed like a large crab claw. "Diamond!" he repeated.

"Oh, it's a *crazy* story. After Sum reported the criminals' breaking in and taking our stuff, including our last bit of cash, some policeman went to the apartment and apparently found a — well — a sparkly stone on the floor.

"Sum's family gave it to her years ago, when she and Dash were married," Early lied, feeling prouder of herself by the moment, "and she'd put it somewhere so safe, she'd lost it. She and Dash couldn't afford to make it into a ring, so she had tucked it away, not feeling it was right to sell a gift like that. The criminals must've knocked it out of its safe hiding place, wherever that was. So now they say Dash was *stealing*, which of course doesn't fit. It'll all get straightened out with some careful spy work and a few questions. The police are great at this kind of thing, aren't they?"

"Yes, yes, sure," Mr. Pincer said. "Didn't hear all this before . . . wonder why . . . the eye of a spy . . . well!" He seemed to shake himself back to the present, and the claw slipped back down behind the desk.

"You're quite a kid to come here, and I'll try to help you, ah, get some *memories* written down. Precious *memories*. Not that your dad won't be back *soon*, of course, yes, *soon*!" He ended with a fake laugh that didn't fit the distracted crease between his eyes.

Early, feeling very successful about having made Mr. Pincer behave in such a guilty way, decided it was time for a bit more pressure. She placed both hands over her face and let her head fall forward. "The way you said *memories*, it was as if my dad wasn't coming home," she said, her voice muffled. "Ever. I heard. *Memories*." She allowed the last word to wobble out in an accusing tone. Her eyes still covered, she said, "I just needed to do something to make everyone remember what a good person my father is. Writing words helps, like my father always said."

There was silence in the room. When she lifted her head, she saw, to her amazement, that she was facing an empty chair. The eye of a spy was right! She'd stopped looking, which was a bad idea. Mr. Pincer could move quickly — and silently. He'd closed the door behind him, but Early opened it a crack.

An angry voice drifted from down the hall. "What's going on here? I'm told one thing, the kid tells me another, another entirely, and this will not happen, I tell you right now, will not! *Not!*"

Early heard a shrill voice respond, a woman's voice. "Gotcha," she said. "We'll see whadda heck is goin' on. Wohnappen again."

Early hugged her notebook to her chest, her mouth opening in a slow O. That way of speaking was familiar.

Should she mention to Mr. Pincer that one of the criminals had a way of speaking she didn't recognize, a mishmash of syllables that sounded just like the accent down the hall?

No, Early thought. She should not.

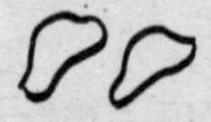

Chase

Moments later, Mr. Pincer propelled her out of his office and around the corner to a small conference room with a rubbery plant in the corner. "Got a few things to take care of, but do make yourself comfortable and I'll send one of your father's coworkers in to chat." He nodded, still wiping absentmindedly at the sticky patch on his forehead. He scuttled around the corner, then ducked back.

"Oh, hungry? Hungry?" he asked.

"Always!" Early said eagerly, although she was still full of pancakes. Tracking down food might keep him busy for a while.

She sat quietly and opened the notebook. Best not to write anything, not yet. Whew, she was glad that she'd seen Mr. Pincer's reaction to the found diamond, and that she'd come up with a distracting story. She was also glad that she hadn't mentioned *The First Book of Rhythms*. Something told her that was a lucky move, something about the way Mr. Pincer had repeated, "All your books . . . All, all . . ." Soon a young man slipped into the room and offered a damp hand. "Mr. Alslip," he said. "One of your father's colleagues. Great guy he was — is — *is*." He had a pink nose and a scraggly mustache, reminding Early of a large rat.

She forced herself to smile. "What exactly did you do with Dash?" Mr. Alslip's mouth fell open. "I didn't mean it *that* way," Early babbled on. "Just, what kinds of things did you talk about?"

"Well, he liked games." Mr. Alslip had recovered and was stroking his mustache.

"What kind of games?" Early asked politely, her pen over the blank page of her notebook.

"Oh, you know, clever puzzles . . . tricky combinations of words and numbers. He enjoyed things that fit unexpectedly."

Mr. Alslip looked uncomfortable. "Yes, that fit." He frowned. "Can't understand . . . gave the hint, spun for fun, add 'n' run, but *then* what, you know?" he muttered to himself. Right then Mr. Pincer stepped into the room. Early realized, with a shock, that he had probably been standing just outside the door. Everything in that office area was carpeted.

"Snack time!" Mr. Pincer said cheerfully, and handed Early a large jelly doughnut. It looked suspiciously like one that had been sitting on his desk when the coffee spilled. The napkin under it was fresh.

"Thanks so much — that's very thoughtful of you," she said. "We were just talking about how much Dash loved puzzles. Like . . ." Early blinked rapidly, as if trying to think back. "Lines in time, for example. Rows of numbers." Mr. Alslip twitched and looked sideways at Mr. Pincer.

"Yes, exactly!" Mr. Pincer said. His hand was now resting on Mr. Alslip's shoulder, which Early thought was odd.

She blinked some more. "Like 1:11. 2:22. You know, that kind of everyday magic."

Mr. Alslip was staring at her. "You *are* like Dash, aren't you?" he blurted, then smiled. "What made —" he began, then stopped. Mr. Pincer's claw was turning white across the knuckles.

"Ow," squeaked Mr. Alslip.

Early pretended she hadn't heard. She yawned. "Well, thanks for sitting down with me, both of you. Mind if I come back tomorrow? Maybe you'll be ready with more details by then. I promise I won't stay long. It just makes me feel good to hear people remembering stuff about my father. If anyone wants to share, I'm there. Anyone!" She waved her arms, hitting the rubbery plant.

It bounced and nodded, but both men were silent. Early had the feeling it was the kind of silence that crackled with unspoken warnings.

Chase

"I'm *good* at this, I'm good, I'm good, I'm *good*!" Early was practically dancing around the Children's Library. *"Gave the hint, spun for fun . . ."* she whispered to herself.

"Good at what, spy-yi-yi-ing?" Jubie dropped the book he'd been looking at and bounced up and down on his seat, his thumbs in the air.

Sum stood, rubbed her eyes, and smiled weakly at the librarian, Mr. Tumble, who was sitting nearby. "It's great to be back here for some new reading material. We've missed coming," she said in a flat tone, gathering an armload of books to check out. "And thanks for helping with the replacement library card and reading to my son."

Early noticed how tired her mother looked that morning, and decided not to tell her about the diamond lie that she'd fed

Mr. Pincer. Sum might sink even lower, not understanding Early's strategy or the fact that Mr. Pincer had indeed snapped at the bait.

"Happy to do it. Come back lots." Mr. Tumble's voice sounded genuine.

"We will." Sum nodded. "Okay, kids. Don't want to miss lunch."

"Yeah, you gotta *wait* when you're *late* and I'm hungry already," Jubie grumbled.

Early, zipping up her jacket, said, "Hey, you made a rhyme! Pretty good, Jubie."

Her brother nodded, looking steadily at Mr. Tumble. "I like you. And I'm a spy. Early's getting us a house, did you know? Gonna surprise Dash!"

"Ahh . . ." The librarian smiled. Early couldn't tell whether he knew their family story or not.

As the three Pearls walked through the door, Mr. Tumble frowned for a moment, pushed his lips out in a tight line as if measuring an idea, then reached for the phone on the corner of his desk.

"I'm calling as you requested," he said slowly.

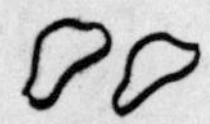

Chase

Sum had a job interview at McDonald's the next day at noon, but had agreed to head back to the library beforehand. Early offered to go on her own that morning, but Sum wouldn't hear of it.

"We three are sticking together, young lady," Sum said. "As long as we leave Harold Washington in a couple of hours. Then you and Jubie can hang out just inside the restaurant entrance while I do my interview, and if I get the job" — Sum sighed and sucked in a huge gulp of air, as if ready to dive underwater — "then maybe we can find a day care close to the library, a nicer one. We'll manage."

"Only if they got trucks and snacks! Only then," Jubie chimed in.

"Only then," Sum agreed.

Sum and Jubie headed for story hour in the Children's Library, as they had the day before, and Early hurried upstairs to the sixth floor. She waved to Mrs. Wormser, who looked around, then gave a quick go-on-in signal. Early slipped through the Staff Only door and walked quietly down the hall toward Mr. Pincer's office.

On the way, she passed a woman she hadn't seen yesterday, someone with fluffy, colorless hair and see-through skin. One large blue vein wiggled down the side of her face, like a river in the wrong place. A plastic sign on her desk read MARY WHISSEL.

"Excuse me," Early said. "Which way is the bathroom?" She mumbled the word *bathroom* so that it came out sounding like *ba-foo.*

The woman was typing on a computer. "Wea?" she asked. Then added, "Onie steaff."

Thrilled by what she'd heard, Early beamed. "Oh, my dad is staff. Wait, I remember! Been there before," she said as she bounced on down the hallway. To her relief, Mary Whissel kept typing.

This time Mr. Pincer was ready for her. His door was closed and locked, and a sign taped above the handle read IN MEETINGS ALL DAY.

Early's shoulders sagged. Walking slowly back toward Ms. Whissel, she said, "Excuse me, but maybe you could help. I'm Dashel Pearl's daughter, and looking for anyone who wants to share some stories about him. We miss him so much, and . . ." Early waited.

The woman didn't react; she continued typing. Early tried another approach. "I met Mr. Alslip yesterday. Is there someone else Dash worked with?"

Ms. Whissel squinted one eye, as if Early were irritating it. "Whassat?" she asked. Yup, no doubt about that accent.

Early whispered, "I think you know what I'm talking about." The woman's eyes clicked into focus and she scowled.

"Git goin'," she said, jerking her head toward the hallway. She turned back to her desk.

"Yes, ma'am," Early said, and then whispered under her breath, "for what *that's* worth." Swinging her arms, she walked a few purposeful steps down the carpeted hall and ducked behind a desk in an empty cubicle around the corner.

She heard Ms. Whissel's chair squeak as if she'd leaned backward. Early held her breath.

"Mr. Pincer, please," the woman said, and cleared her throat while waiting.

"Hello, yes." She paused. "Yes, she sure is. You goddit. Yes, put ta word out. Very good." The chair squeaked again and all was quiet except for the soft clacking of computer keys. Early was just getting ready to pop out and scurry down the hall, when she heard a *creak-shwump-swish-swish* and the woman's legs swept by. Early watched the shiny stockings vanish. All was quiet. She jumped up and ducked into Ms. Whissel's cubicle to see what she'd been typing. If she got caught, Early could pretend she was going for tissues.

Her heart pounding, she leaned close and read an e-mail directed to all employees of History and Social Sciences:

FOR SECURITY REASONS, AS YOU HEARD IN A MEETING LAST WEEK, YOU MAY NOT DISCUSS ANYTHING TO DO WITH DASHEL PEARL WITH ANY VISITORS TO THE LIBRARY. IF YOU HAVE QUESTIONS OR NEW INFORMATION, PLEASE CONTACT MR. PINCER.

Early hugged her notebook and scurried down another branch of the hallway. It ended in a door. Taking a deep breath, she turned the knob and pulled.

She was facing a small, brightly lit room lined floor to ceiling with books. A number of file cabinets divided the space. The Limited Access room!

Dash had once brought her here, explaining that this was where high-security books and articles were kept. They were never checked out, as they might not come back. This was where you'd come to read about crimes, murders, drugs, gangs, stuff like that. Dash said that folks on both sides of the law did research there.

Early thought about that as she looked around.

One wall was glass and faced the open stacks of the sixth floor. In the middle of this wall was the public entrance door, behind the librarians' counter. Several adults, seated at long wooden tables in the center of the room, bent low over piles of books and papers. All was quiet. Early was wondering how on earth she could blend in when she spotted Mr. Waive's ears.

He was crouched over a screen in the corner, his finger following fine lines of print. Early tiptoed across the room. When she hit a squeak in the floor, Mr. Waive looked up, but only from the side of his eye.

The grin-frown was back. "What took you so long?" he asked, in that raspy whisper. "Been waiting."

Catch, *from the Middle English* cacchen

Verb: to capture or seize; to discover with surprise; to lead astray by twisting the truth; to pick up, as with germs; to see.

Noun: a tricky or unsuspected situation; a prize worth having.

2

Catch

Mr. Waive pointed at the screen. "Chicago crime rings. Al Capone and his buddies. One of the specialties of your father's department and most of the collection is right here. As you know, this city has a long, distinguished history of gangsters, thieves, smugglers, clever frauds, and forgeries. Unexplained disappearances. Your father is just one in a long list of missing people. Fascinating, I must say!"

Early sat down at the computer next to Mr. Waive and opened her notebook. "Mr. Wa —" she began.

He rushed on, "If anyone asks, you're with me. I'm your teacher, and you're doing a project on Chicago crime. Got it?"

She nodded again. "Mr. Waive, there's bad news. About Dash."

This time he looked directly at her. Careful to keep her voice just above a whisper, she told him right away about the discovery of the diamond, giving him the Pincer version.

While Early spoke, Mr. Waive bowed his head and placed his hands together over his mouth, as if praying. After she'd finished, he remained in that position. Silence.

Finally he raised his head and asked softly, "You sure that diamond story is the best you can do?"

Early's heart beat fast, and panicky sweat prickled on her neck. *Now* what? Bad idea, lying to Mr. Waive; of *course* he'd seen through it.

She swallowed, a loud *ga-glump* sound, and muttered, "Well, no, sorry about that. I was just trying to stick with what the police told Sum to do, that is, keep quiet about where the stone came from, but . . ." Early then shared all that she knew.

Mr. Waive's eyebrows went up and down, but he said nothing. When she'd finished, he reached across her, turned on her computer, and typed *Antwerp diamond heist 2003* into the search bar, did the same on his computer, and sat back. "Let's start here," he said. "First thing to do is learn about the crime."

The next ten minutes were quiet while both of them read. Early couldn't help wondering what Dash would think of all this: a mysterious, sparkly gemstone from the biggest diamond theft *ever*, and found in their apartment! And she, Early, sitting next to Mr. Waive in the Limited Access room and reading about where that diamond had been.

The facts were hard to absorb. On that fateful February night so many years ago, thousands of cut and uncut diamonds, bars of gold, loose gemstones, and pieces of jewelry were stolen from a vault in the Antwerp Diamond Center, a business thought to be one of the most secure in the world. This was an ingenious crime, one in which layers of security cameras and alarms were silently disabled. A vault with a code that was thought to be unbreakable was entered and exited as if by magic. Of 160 locked storage units, 123 were emptied overnight. The criminals left a trail of dropped stones, watches, and rolling pearls in their haste to carry off a giant load.

Many questions remain unanswered, both about how this

crime was carried out and whether all involved were caught. Four Italian men eventually went to prison, all members of a professional group of criminals known as the School of Turin. Each had a special capability. With nicknames like the King of Keys, the Genius, the Monster, and Speedy, they soon caught the imagination of the press. Those who were arrested haven't revealed their methods in any believable way, but admitted that years went into preparation and planning.

The four were only traced because of trash dumped hurriedly in woods by the side of a road as the thieves sped away the following morning. Someone who walked often around this property found the pile that very day. Eventually, arrests were made based on DNA collected from a partly eaten salami sandwich and a bit of tape used to wrap one of the vault cameras; receipts from a grocery store near the criminals' Antwerp rental; and faces recorded on neighborhood store surveillance cameras. One easily recognizable diamond — a huge and valuable certified stone from the Diamond Center vault — was found in the Italian home of one of the thieves after he was finally taken into custody. Aside from tiny gems stuck to the garbage and this one stone, however, the thousands of cut and uncut diamonds that were stolen on that extraordinary February day had yet to be found. The estimated value was staggering: between 100 and 140 million dollars.

"After this week, once the news gets out, they'll have to rewrite the account," muttered Mr. Waive. "Now that a stone from the most famous heist ever has turned up in Chicago, the FBI will be all over the city like kids on Halloween candy. Amazing story, huh?"

"Kind of like a made-up mystery," Early agreed. "And Dash has somehow been dragged into all this, which is awful. But *why*? Why would anyone want to hurt a guy like Dash?"

"I doubt they would, but it's possible that he simply made the wrong move at a fateful moment. Maybe he stumbled into it. Stepped in on the wrong beat. Any clues might have been impossible to comprehend from his vantage point."

Early, storing the words *comprehend* and *vantage point* away for later, scrambled to add something valuable. Mr. Waive had a way of making you want to catch what he thought you could. After he suggested they check out any possible relationship between books and smuggling, she scrolled down page after page of references, learning an odd assortment of facts. For instance, stolen books, even rare ones, were often hard to trace. Shipments of old volumes had been used to hide paper money, bills tucked between the pages. Older books often had stronger bindings than newer ones and therefore lasted longer. Next, she found directions on how to transform an old novel into a box by cutting a hole in the center, underneath the cover so no one could tell; the outside edges of the pages were then artfully glued shut so nothing could fall out. Large pieces of jewelry, antique coins, and gold nuggets had been successfully smuggled in that way.

"Awesome," Early murmured, and when Mr. Waive leaned over to read, she noticed his shirt collar had holes in it and that he smelled like the liquid soap used in the shelter bathrooms.

"But the volumes in Dash's boxes," she continued, "were mostly thin. No room for secret compartments." She paused. "Hey, even though he looked through each one when he was making his lists, maybe he missed something. Could be the diamond was stuffed into the inside crack of a binding, got loose, and fell out in our apartment. Then Dash never knew it was there, and the guys thought he'd taken it."

"You might be onto something," Mr. Waive muttered. "Let's talk later. Hurry, because I doubt you're welcome here. And don't look so excited."

Early, now looking for *stolen or smuggled diamonds*, scrolled as fast as she could and had just hit a page that she felt was valuable, a page explaining that stolen diamonds were easy to sell or *launder*, whatever that meant, when a hand bounced her chair backward.

"Mr. Pincer!" She smiled sweetly. He was trying to read the screen over her shoulder, she could tell, but she'd already clicked it closed. "How nice to see you here!" The claw let go, and she spun around to face him.

"No unaccompanied children in the reading room, I'm afraid," he said. "Afraid, no, well, not that." He cleared his throat. "Have to go now. You. Go."

Early blinked and smiled again. "This is my homeschooling teacher, Mr. Waive. I'm doing a project on international crime rings. Quite a few, I must say! Never knew there were so many ways of getting things past the police. Of course, as Dash always told me, only losers steal instead of earn, but it's history, so it's important to know!"

"Ah, yes," Mr. Waive growled, over one shoulder. "This is a public space, of course, and I'm the accompanying adult. I'm quite sure this child has a library card." He cleared his throat as if that settled things and he was too busy to be disturbed.

"I see," Mr. Pincer said, his tone about as friendly as an ice cube. "See, yes. History and *rumpa-rumpa*." He coughed, struggled to finish his sentence, and ended up with a strangled "cri-cri-*mpa*!"

Early couldn't resist saying, "Bit of doughnut caught in your throat? I *hate* that. Can I help?" and reached around to pat his back.

Mr. Pincer leapt away, one hand chopping the air, and scuttled back through the same door Early had found. His coughs trailed into the distance.

"Be cautious about playing with that one," Mr. Waive leaned over to say. "Never humiliate a dangerous animal; it won't forget. Believe me, I know. And so may your father."

"Ohhh." Early suddenly felt terrible. "Think I've done something bad?"

"Not at all. Refused to be bullied. Good sign. Keep going."

Early did, and wondered why it was a sign and where she was headed.

2

Catch

"I lied, too," Mr. Waive said in the elevator on the way down to the Children's Library an hour later. "Used to doing it, I guess.

Embarrassed. Lost my home also, a couple of years ago. I think I told you I took my sister and her family in after I'd retired and she got sick. Well, I kept paying her bills, and by the time she died, it was all gone." He shrugged and scowled, as though he wanted to be sure Early didn't feel sorry for him.

"Wow," Early said. "I thought you smelled familiar."

Mr. Waive looked sharply at her. This was the first time she'd seen him look off balance.

"Like shelter soap."

He grinned. "Natural-born sleuth. Your father's girl."

Early smiled back. Suddenly Mr. Waive didn't seem quite so scary, and he was using fewer big words. It was almost, with Mr. Waive, like the big words were his way of building a protective fence. Syllables to hide behind.

Sitting on a bench outside the door to the Children's Library, Mr. Waive listened intently while Early told him about her attempts to interview Dash's coworkers yesterday. Both the visiting supervisor and Mr. Alslip had been nervous. Very.

It was as Early said Mr. Alslip's name out loud that she made her discovery — one word hiding within another.

"Alslip. *Al*slip. Alslip could be Al!" Early said.

Mr. Waive nodded. "I wouldn't be surprised if that were so." Then he was quiet for a moment. "The gang with masks, they took every last book in your apartment?"

Early hesitated for a moment, then said, "Except for one kids' book that fell under a broken table. We have it. Langston Hughes's *The First Book of Rhythms*."

"Ahhh!" Mr. Waive's face lit up, making him look almost happy. The wrinkles in his cheeks deepened farther, bunching around a huge smile. "My old friend!"

"Dash used to recite the poem to us that starts 'If 2 and 2 are 4.' He said you taught it to him. If he's trying to figure out something, he sometimes says, 'What's the rhythm, Langston?'"

"Ahhh, that is wonderful to hear." Mr. Waive's eyebrows had zoomed up his forehead. "My fault, I should have tried to find your father after he left my school. I always remembered his brilliance, you know, and wondered what he was up to, but I guess problems of my own intervened."

Brilliance . . . the criminals who had carried out the Antwerp crime had been described as brilliant, and Early pushed away the connection in her mind. She focused on *intervened*, realizing Mr. Waive was building a fence again. "'Problems' is the name of that poem, you know," she said.

"Exactly," Mr. Waive wheezed. "And to finish my thought about your father, it isn't that easy to stay in touch with a student who is growing up in foster homes. Amazing that he got himself so far."

"Is *going* so far," Early corrected with a flash of panic, sure that Mr. Waive hadn't meant to say it in the past tense. The man was such an exact thinker. Why was he talking about Dash as if he wasn't coming back?

Early hurried on, blotting the worry with words. "You and I will figure out who has forced him into hiding. *Coercion* of some kind." She hoped Mr. Waive noticed her use of that *C* word, one that sounded as sticky and gluey as what it meant.

But Mr. Waive only coughed a long, painful cough, and nodded. Early tried chatting with him more, but he didn't respond.

"Want to meet back here tomorrow, Mr. Waive?" she asked. "Seems like we both have time."

"Research rhythms," he rasped, stepping into the elevator. At least Early *thought* that was what he said. Or was it "Please search rhythms"? Mr. Waive's voice was so worn and scratchy, it was sometimes hard to hear.

"Hey!" Early called. "That's so *weird*; that's something my father said to me," as the door closed on her words.

2

Catch

Sum interviewed for the job at McDonald's while Early and Jubie sat on a stack of papers inside the door. Early read a library book aloud to her brother. The smells were intoxicating.

Finally Jubie, who'd been warned to stay quiet, piped up, "Hey, Early! How about we ask those kids over there for a few fries while we're waiting for Sum! Can we do that? Looks like they're done, look, they're throwing stuff away."

Early whispered, "Maybe if Sum gets a job, she can bring us back some McDonald's food every day. How about *that*?"

"Yeah!" The thought was too much, and Jubie bounced to his feet, patting his stomach, sticking out his tongue, and panting like a dog. "I'm starved! *Starved!* Hurry up, Sum!"

Early pulled him back down just as a load of teenagers piled in the door, and Jubie called to them, "I'm hungry! Gimme fries!" and grinned.

One waved, then a few minutes later, handed him a paper napkin with a pile of fries on it. "Thanks!" shouted Jubie. "We was *hungry*!"

"Uh-oh," Early said. Someone behind the counter was shaking her head at Sum and pointing to Jubie.

Sum didn't get the job. Early was afraid she'd be angry, but she wasn't. Just sad.

That day after lunch — shelter sandwiches that tasted much less yummy than McDonald's food — Early sat on one of the bunks and started planning.

Dash's heart kept a rhythm with her own at all times, and his power, drive, and sparkle filled her mind. They'd find him, of course, but meanwhile she also needed to continue Dash's work on finding them a *home*, a place to go and grow, as he used to say.

Sum didn't look strong enough to stay in this shelter forever. Although there were moments when she seemed like her old self, she was losing her hold. Sometimes Early felt kind of queasy about having lied, disobeying her mother about sharing the diamond news. First, one version with Mr. Pincer and then the truth with Mr. Waive, but both had felt necessary. This was a strategy, and the Pearl family needed strategies. Badly. Early looked over at her mother, who lay on the bunk with her eyes closed. *Hold fast, Sum,* Early said silently. *Hold fast to dreams. For Dash.*

There was no sign that Sum got her message. Jubie was busily driving his blue truck back and forth over his mother's feet, making *brrrrt* sounds, but she didn't seem to notice.

Early wondered what the best way might be to catch the attention of a grown-up, a busy person with power to help. Someone like the mayor. Or President Obama, a guy who loved Chicago and must have seen some of the thousands of empty houses dotting the neighborhoods in his city. Both had kids. Both had a home here. Then she thought of her teacher at the Hughes School, Ms. Chaff, and the way she'd dabbed at her nose after Early read aloud her description of how she'd fix up their dream house in Woodlawn.

An idea as small as the dot on a question mark appeared in her mind. A dot of dazzling light. Out of habit, she did what Dash had taught her to do: Spin it around, look at it from all sides, try to find the weak spot, if there was one. There didn't seem to be one; the dot was rapidly exploding into a thrilling thought. Early clapped her hands, a loud crack of joy, startling both Jubie and Sum. "That's it!" she shouted, bouncing to her feet. "Simple! I need all the kids! We can do this, we *can*!" And even though she was eleven, she jumped up and down, her snow boots making a *squish-scree* sound against the linoleum.

She could hardly wait for the tutoring room to open that afternoon. She'd start there.

2

Catch

Most tutors at Helping Hand were college students. They probably would have enjoyed just hanging out with the kids, but their main job was to help with homework. Many kids at the shelter didn't *want* to do more schoolwork as soon as they'd finished a long day. Most struggled at their grade level, having moved a bunch of times, and had grown to hate everything about school. What they really wanted was a place to play ball or run around outside, but that wasn't a choice.

Early understood their reluctance; it was hard enough to change schools and neighborhoods, but to leave everything familiar and then be labeled as one of the "shelter kids" was doubly tough. You stood out and might never fit in, not easily. More fortunate kids were often afraid of head lice and germs, as Mrs. Happadee had explained to her. Hiding the fact of homelessness was clearly best for peaceful survival in a classroom, but the idea felt nasty. Like losing your home was a dirty secret. No wonder these kids didn't want to think about school once they'd left the building.

Everyone looked more cheerful when a special visitor came to the tutoring room, maybe an artist or writer, and the homework was put aside for a day. Once, a painter came and helped them make a mural on the tutoring-room wall. Early thought this was the key to getting people excited about what she wanted to do. It could be a project!

As soon as Mr. John unlocked the door that afternoon, she and Jubie burst inside the room. Only two other kids followed, and Early had never seen them before. *They must be new to the shelter. Oh, well,* Early thought. *There'll be a bigger group on other days.*

Mr. John introduced them. "Isobel and Marcus, meet Early and Jubie. Hey, you guys are both sister-brother combos!"

The four kids looked at one another; Early thought Isobel might be close to her age, and Marcus and Jubie, who were about the same size, were already unloading a box of crayons and setting themselves up at the table for coloring.

"So . . ." Mr. John rubbed his hands together. "Anyone got homework? I know you're not in school yet here, Isobel . . . and you're doing your own thing right now, Early. How's that going?"

"Great!" Early beamed. "In fact, I have a fantastic idea. A *big* idea. A project that kids in all the shelters could work on. A way to get us all back into homes."

Mr. John blinked and smiled. "Sounds amazing," he said. "How would you do it?"

Early first described going by train to the Harold Washington Library, and seeing all the abandoned houses and apartment buildings. "I remember them in my old neighborhood, too. They were there, but I never thought about it because my family *had* a home then."

Isobel nodded. "Yeah, we had a home, too. But we been in shelters a couple of years now. We dream about having a place of our own again," she said. "*Ooh*, my mom, boy, does she want that!"

"Us, too! Us, too!" said Early.

Mr. John was nodding.

"So, what's your idea?" Isobel asked. She'd crossed her arms and tapped one foot, as if Early couldn't possibly have a solution to such a big problem.

"Well, we'll need some drugstore cameras, a way to get around, and maybe some help with spelling and writing. Oh, and some stamps and envelopes."

Early described her idea: The tutors at all of the shelters around the city would organize short field trips in which they'd walk or drive through neighborhoods, and the kids could snap pictures of abandoned houses that they thought should be rescued.

Then, once the pictures were printed, the kids would take the photos they liked best and describe what that house or apartment would look like, in detail, if it were theirs to keep. If they could *adopt* it with their family, fix it up, and make it into a home again — kind of like the game the Pearls used to play when looking at the house with the cat.

"You *imagine* yourself into the home," Early explained. "You picture yourself doing stuff in the bedroom, peeking out the front door, deciding what color the walls and curtains should be, making cookies or having a birthday party, and running around in the yard."

Then they'd clip the building photo to the description, add a picture of the dreamer, and collect a big stack of these dreams from every family shelter in the city of Chicago. They'd end up with hundreds! Thousands! Copies would be mailed to famous people who might be able to help.

"Ta-da!" Early exclaimed, throwing out her arms. "Then powerful folks will know about our hopes!"

Isobel clapped, and Mr. John was rubbing his hands together. "It's quite a thought and simple to do, with the right permissions. It's hard to say what will happen, but why not try?" He promised to bring it up with his supervisor later that day.

Early and Isobel spent the rest of their time in the tutoring room, drawing pictures of houses and describing the rooms inside.

"Don't forget the rugs! Soft and squishy on your toes!" Isobel was drawing lots of small lines to show a thick rug. "And I like to clean, so I'll be washing and polishing! My home won't *know* itself, it's gonna be so fresh!"

"Yeah, and maybe one day I'll even have a solid bed, one with a piece of wood at the top and the bottom! I never had a bed off the floor except for the bunks here." Early was busily drawing a bed with legs, posts, and a puffy green comforter.

"And maybe pillows that feel good," Isobel added. "And mattresses that don't have all that plastic covering and bug spray on them."

"Uh-*huh*." Early nodded, then thought about what Isobel had said. "That why the beds smell so nasty?"

"Better than getting vermin," Isobel said, coloring her kitchen table a cheerful orange. "All the shelters gotta do that."

"Oh," Early said. "How many shelters have you stayed in?"

Isobel paused and looked at the ceiling, counting on her fingers. Early liked the way she took the time to make her point, whatever it might be. "Eight," she said, and nodded her head dramatically. "And that is a *lot* of moving," she added.

"Yeah," Early said. "Sure is. Time for a home!" She grinned.

"I like you," Isobel said, her head on one side. "You're my kind of girl. Want to be best shelter friends? For as long as we're both here?"

"Yeah," Early said again. She hadn't smiled this much in a long time.

When the tutoring room closed that day, all four kids continued talking on their way up the stairs.

"Catch you later," Isobel said as she and her brother headed on up to their room.

"Later," Early said, jerking her chin upward in a crisp, got-lots-to-do gesture.

Velma was seated at one of the long tables, sewing a button on the neck of her winter coat. After watching the kids, she nodded and smiled. "Told her," she muttered to herself. "That kid's going places, gonna help her mama," she said. "Kids, they got less con*fuuu*-sion in their brains."

A woman who was new to the shelter looked over. "Waddid you say? Hoozat?" she asked.

Velma looked over at the woman, noticed she had nice sneakers and a fancy jacket on, and shrugged.

Cover, *from the Middle English* coveren *and Latin* cooperire

Verb: to hide, protect, or conceal; to place something over or around an object or living thing so as to shield from danger; to guard from attack.

Noun: something that shelters or disguises; a situation providing protection from enemies; the front or back of the binding on a book.

Cover

After a week of sun and wispy clouds, the snow had started again: a wet, heavy white that covered cars, streetlights, hoods, and hats. It fell without wind to carry it, the flakes so dense that it was hard to see far.

Early had a miserable time rousing Sum the next morning, but finally got the three of them dressed, fed, and onto the train to Harold Washington.

"How many days you going to make us do this, Early Pearl?" Sum asked, her voice grumpy. "I love you doing research and I love all your plans, but this is a long trip for me and Jubie every day. I'm afraid I fell asleep in a corner of the Children's Library yesterday when he was playing, and the librarian, that nice Mr. Tumble, woke me and asked if I was okay. I said, 'No, would you be okay if you'd lost your partner, all your money, and your home?' Guess I should've smiled and said yes, but I'm getting too worn out to do that these days."

Early looked at her mother's face. She had pockets under her eyes, like the skin had gotten tired of holding on in the last few weeks. Like life was rushing her away from being young.

"Sum." Early patted her arm gently. "Mr. Waive and I are finding out good stuff. We're getting someplace; we're gonna *find* Dash! And Mr. John, the tutor in our shelter, really likes my ideas. He's all excited about working on them. We got things happening, so we all need to hold fast. Just picture Dash telling you what to do, and you'll feel stronger!"

It didn't work. Sum covered her eyes with one hand and sat still, but her mouth was crying. Early and Jubie both looked at her, and people on the train looked, too. Then Sum said softly, patting at her eyes with the end of her scarf, "I'm so sorry, I really am. I'm trying. I just feel lost. I need Dash so badly. Guess I never realized how empty life could get without him. But I'm trying."

Early didn't say any more and squeezed her mother's hand. Jubie leaned his head against her on the other side. "You got us, and we'll be good," he said. "I won't whine no more."

Sum gave him a sad smile. "You mean *any*more."

"*Any*more," chirped Jubie.

I gotta be strong, Early thought to herself. *Strong enough for three. Just like Dash was strong enough for four.*

She gazed out, not really paying attention to what she saw. A boy carried a puppy across the street; a school bus stopped to pick up kids waiting on a corner in front of another big shelter, which Sum had pointed out to Early the other day. And then Early saw a man in a big jacket, his shoulders hunched, walk from between two buildings. Limping, he moved slowly toward the line of kids.

The side of his face . . . it looked just like Dash! Dash, Dash, *Dash!* This flash seen from a moving train, an impression lasting only a second, shot her bolt upright in her seat. She glanced at

Sum, wondering if she should say something. Sum's eyes were closed. Jubie was busy playing with his truck.

"Rrrt, ka-ka-brt, brrt!" he muttered, driving it back and forth on his leg.

No, Early thought. *I've been thinking of Dash so much that now I'm seeing him. I'm just seeing what I want to see. Inventing things.*

Early squeezed her eyes shut for a moment, forcing herself to concentrate on the sound of the train grinding over the tracks, metal on metal.

She opened her eyes to see a boarded-up building they'd noticed before, one with a red roof, fly by outside the train window. This morning the roof had a gentle mound of white on top of its chimney and looked promising beneath the snow.

The train screeched to a stop at Harold Washington. Stepping out onto the cold platform with her silent mother and brother, she felt painfully alone.

Cover

Mr. Waive wasn't there this morning. Early peeked through the glass door of the Limited Access room, but was afraid to enter on her own.

She knew it was no good trying to get information out of Mr. Pincer or the lady with the blue vein. But Mr. Alslip! *Al.* If she could spot him coming or going . . . she *knew* he had something to tell her. He'd had that eager look on his face and Mr. Pincer had stopped him.

Pulling off her coat, she sat down at one of the tables for the general public and opened her notebook. She'd found a seat near the open stacks, one partly hidden by books but with a clear view of the front desk and Staff Only door. She pulled a few thick books out of a nearby shelf and made herself a little wall. She opened one of the books, as if reading, and slunk down in her chair.

A man with a bow tie and crooked glasses went into the Limited Access room. Next, a woman with a fur collar on her coat. Now two students who looked about the same age as Mr. John. Then Mr. Pincer appeared from nowhere — *oh, no!*

Early slid even lower. The supervisor was walking next to a man who resembled a large chimpanzee, all fuzziness and a big, heavy forehead; it was difficult to look away. Luckily, Mr. Pincer seemed just as fascinated by him. They disappeared through the Staff Only door.

It was already after ten and Early was losing hope. She'd have to meet Sum and Jubie in time to get back to the shelter for lunch. And then *whoosh!* Mr. Alslip strode past, pushing a cart of books.

"Psst! Mr. Alslip!" she whispered as he hurried by. He glanced in her direction, and his eyes flickered with recognition and something else — was it fear? He wriggled his shoulders as if they could hide him, and kept moving.

Early thought he had jerked his head to the right. She followed, trotting after his cart as it zoomed down a long, straight corridor of books.

People, she realized, had rhythms, too. Unique ways of behaving and talking. If she could read Mr. Alslip's rhythms, what would they tell her?

Cover

"I can't talk to you!" was the first thing he whispered. "This is dangerous stuff, *very* dangerous, and if I'm seen talking to you, I'll be fired and — and maybe killed. We might *both* be," he squeaked.

"What?" Early whispered back. "Are you kidding? *Killed?*" The word had a dreadful, stony sound, and it felt wrong even to say it.

Mr. Alslip was still moving quickly, looking on all sides, pausing, turning a corner, rolling his cart farther and farther from the offices at the center of the floor. Finally he stopped at a U-shaped study area with heavy chairs and a wraparound shelf for a table.

"You wait here," he ordered. "Duck under, pull a chair close, and we'll park the cart in front. There. You're gone."

What would Sum say? Early wondered, but she already knew: *Are you crazy? Hiding in a faraway part of the sixth floor with a man you don't know?* The thing was, it was now or maybe never, and she needed to ask some questions. Early nodded.

He scurried a few steps away, paused to listen, and hurried back, his shoes making a *shree-shree* sound on the bare floors.

"We've got to whisper," he began, dropping into a chair on the other side of the book cart. "Jeez, my heart is pounding." He paused, one hand on his chest. "This whole thing is nuts. Sorry about frightening you, but it's a dangerous time." He took a deep breath and blew it out in puffs, as if making invisible smoke rings.

"That's okay. Thanks for talking to me," Early whispered.

Mr. Alslip dusted off his shoes, rubbing one foot at a time on the back of his pant legs, which seemed to calm him. "Actually, I was hoping you'd come back to the library. You're a brave kid and there are things I want to tell you.

"First, your dad didn't do anything wrong. At least, I don't think so. And if something happens to me and I disappear, too, at least you'll know the truth. Or, more accurately, what I can tell you. Sometimes it's hard to say what's true and what's not, especially when no one leaves prints. Hey — get it?" Mr. Alslip glanced at Early. "A foot and a book can both leave a print, though the number's the thing . . . sorry, can't help myself!"

"Are you the guy my father called Al?" she asked. "The guy who liked playing games with him?"

"That's me," he said.

"I knew it!" Early crowed, in a loud whisper. "Mr. Pincer told the police there's no Al here and that Mr. Lyman Scrub doesn't exist."

"Really?" Al asked, his whiskers twitching. "Lovely. Good to know he's watching my back."

Early paused. "So you're saying Mr. Pincer is a part of all this, too?"

"No, well, maybe, but not as far as Dash knew, at least I think. Forget I said that! Okay, let's stick to the skinny. Here's how your father and I fell into all this: One day a man approached me in the stacks, where I was shelving books. He gave me his card, which said *Lyman Scrub, Bookseller.*"

Early nodded. What was the *skinny*?

"He explained that he needed two reliable pages who wanted to make a bit of money and were 'coming up' in the library world."

"Yes, I already know this. Dash told us," Early interrupted, worried that he wouldn't finish before someone found them.

"How do you have *any* idea what I'm going to say?" Al snapped, his nose and chin now twitching independently, a rare feat on one face.

"Sorry," Early whispered. "Go on."

"This Scrub fellow explained that he worked with some people from the New York City area whose job was to store, pack, and then sell unwanted estate donations, some of them junk. You know, old books no one could want."

Early nodded, thinking that the way her father talked about out-of-print books made them glow, as if they were objects deserving respect. This man was no Dash.

Al was now pulling busily on his mustache. "So, we did the job, each taking on separate parts of it. I'm living in my brother's house right now and didn't want to give the address, so your father got the cartons at his apartment and I picked them up, along with a list of what was inside. I delivered them to an address in Marquette Park, one I wasn't supposed to tell your father."

Early nodded again. This was a beat, all right: She could feel what was coming. "It sounds like you thought there was something suspicious about the whole business from the start," she said. "Too bad —"

"I'm just a more cautious fellow than your father. More to hide. And don't drop snippy hints with me, young lady. I don't have to tell you a thing, you know."

"Sorry, please go on," Early said. Could guilt and fear be parts of the same rhythm?

"Mr. Scrub paid us generously, instructing me to give your father his share after each pickup. And then one evening when I came by, Dash told me that he had kept one of the books. For you kids. He said he'd paid more than enough for it, having checked on its value, and had put a star next to it on the list. I had the box in my arms.

"Setting it down, I asked, 'You think that's a good idea?'

"Your father shrugged off any worries, explaining to me that he was just making the process easier for Mr. Scrub. He gave me a small envelope with the money for the book, and asked me to give it to the people who received the box when I dropped it off.

"Here's the part I'm feeling like I want you to know: I didn't give the money to the guys who took the delivery. They were big men, looked kinda rough, and I was afraid. I could picture one of them punching me in the nose before I'd even had a chance to explain, and seriously, all you have to do is come near my nose and it hurts. Old injury.

"So I never told Dash that I'd taken the envelope home, although I meant to. Time went by, and . . . I stuffed it in a drawer. I convinced myself that Dash was right, no one would mind, and I'd explain I'd forgotten if anyone asked about the missing book.

"A couple of weeks passed. Nothing. We processed more boxes of books. Then one of the guys from the warehouse called my cell phone early one morning and asked if I was the man who had gone through that box of books, the one with a star on the list. I said no, that it had been my colleague, Dashel Pearl. And something in his voice just got me scared. I didn't say a word, either about the missing book or the money Dash had handed me to give them. I know, I know, I should have!

"Later that day I saw Mr. Scrub talking in a low voice with Mr. Pincer in the stacks, although they didn't see me. I didn't tell Dash, maybe feeling guilty about how I'd handled the whole keeping-a-book thing, but I decided to give your father the address of the warehouse and then tell him what I'd done. Or *hadn't* done. Maybe he could drop off the envelope and run. So, I dropped clues about the building number by pointing out time patterns that shared the information in code; he and I liked that kind of brain twister. I was planning to give him the street name the next day. But before I could tell him . . ."

"My father disappeared!" Early blurted, unable to stay quiet for another second. *Guilty,* she thought. He said it himself.

"Shhhh!" Mr. Alslip hissed, leaning close. Early got a whiff of cheesy garlic.

She made a face, no longer caring if that was rude, and hissed back, "So if you were afraid of these guys and Dash suddenly vanished after that weird accident, why didn't you call the police?"

Al shuddered. "I can't say. Perhaps instinct. But I am sorry about your father. . . ."

"Instinct! To save yourself while an entire family is destroyed? Have you ever lost your father, your home, and — and — your whole world? Have you ever lived in a shelter? You aren't sorry enough!" Early spat, itching to punch that twitchy nose herself.

For the first time, Al looked truly upset.

"So can you give *me* the address?" Early asked quickly.

"Don't dare," he said. "But I did drive out there to the warehouse to look, a couple of days after your father vanished. Seemed to me like everyone had gone, no signs of life."

"So why can't you share the address *now*?"

"Can't. Just can't."

Early was dying to shout at him that he was a rat, jump out from behind the cart and run directly to the police, but forced herself to ask calmly, "So, Mr. Alslip, what do you think this whole book business was about? I mean, why the scary guys and everything?"

Al was blinking his eyes rapidly, as if thinking something through. "Maybe the books were being used to *hide* something much more valuable," he said.

"Like how?" Early asked, blinking also.

"I know, crazy idea," Al said, with a split-second smile. His two front teeth were much bigger than the rest. "You can't hide much in a carton of old books that some middleman looks through." He shrugged. "Not exactly secure."

As Early wondered about the easy way he'd said "some middleman," he asked, "Why did you mention rows of numbers the other day? When Mr. Pincer came into the room."

"Why not? Dash used to play around with ideas all the time. Especially, oh, the repeating numbers on the clock."

"Really," Al said. "What a coincidence. And then there was the terrible raid at your place," he said slowly. "Horrible. Everything, huh?"

"Just about," Early said.

"Anything the thieves didn't find?"

What, was he reading her mind? Early looked away.

"Well," she said innocently, "it was hard to see in the mess they left. They destroyed everything and we had to leave that night. I remember one guy had a strong accent that sounded just like Ms. Whissel's."

"Hmm, really!" Mr. Alslip was pulling on his mustache again. "Mr. Pincer's personal assistant, came a day or two after he did. Funny thing, coincidence —"

Just then they heard heavy footsteps approaching, and Early pressed her forehead into her knees. Mr. Alslip jumped to his feet.

"Alslip?" Mr. Pincer's voice sounded angry. "What're you doing back here?"

"Sorting," Mr. Alslip said, his voice sounding exhausted. "Straightening the mess, bunch of books pulled without rhyme or reason."

"Rhyme, I see, ra-*hem*!" Mr. Pincer cleared his throat. "I want you in my office. *Now!* We've got news."

Mr. Pincer stormed away. Early knew she didn't have much time. She had to take the rhythms that fed Al's panic — the guilt, the history with Dash, his habit of hiding — and make them the biggest rhythms he could hear.

"You were his friend," she said. "The guy my father called Al. I know you don't want to get in any more trouble. But I know you don't want to see our family hurt even more. You *have* to tell the police what you know."

"Then I'll be the next to disappear!" Al said.

Early thought about that.

"Not if you find a way to tell them without really telling them," she said. "Not if it looks to the bad guys like you've been caught."

Those were the last words Early got out before Mr. Pincer yelled again, and Mr. Alslip slipped away, moving with the speed of a small animal used to avoiding traps.

Cover

A blank Post-it note was stuck to the table where Early had left her notebook and winter coat. Both were gone. Across the top of the note, in black print, was: *From the desk of Wade Pincer.*

Her heart sank. It was almost time to pick up Sum and Jubie from the Children's Library, and she needed that jacket. Trying to remember exactly what she'd written in the notebook, she was glad that Mr. Waive had reminded her not to record anything secret. He was a smart man.

Slipping through the Staff Only door, she walked slowly toward Mr. Pincer's office. The door was closed. Ms. Whissel was not at her desk. Early could hear a buzz of voices. She took another couple of steps, then realized the buzz was getting fainter. But if she backed up, she could make out some words from inside the room where she'd met Mr. Alslip.

Early ducked in and looked up at the wall. There it was: a metal vent. She froze, willing her heart to stop thudding so loudly.

"Stay out . . . serious . . . danger." From the snatches of urgent-sounding talk, she separated out Mr. Pincer's voice, Mr. Alslip's, and Ms. Whissel's. And then there was a long, gravelly cough. Mr. Waive! What was *he* doing in there? Mr. Pincer must be trying to force some information out of him! Early felt responsible; she'd pulled Mr. Waive into this, after all. She then had the tiniest flash of doubt about Mr. Waive, a question as quick as the sparkle of a snowflake. She pushed it away. Everything she'd learned was making her see *everyone* as possibly hiding something they shouldn't. It would be terrible, she decided at that moment, to live the life of a spy.

A door opened, and Early heard Mr. Waive cough again.

"You've been warned," Mr. Pincer said. "You are not to re-enter this building. Not, not, er, ever again." The door slammed shut and Early heard footsteps moving off down the hallway and the growly rumble of Mr. Waive clearing his throat.

Early was dying to follow him and ask what had happened. But what if the conversation between Mr. Pincer, Mr. Alslip, and the others wasn't over? They might *really* spill the beans, now that Mr. Waive was gone.

She listened closely again.

"Located *blurbledy blurb* ice *blurbledy* a slip . . ." Slipping on ice! Were they talking about the accident?

And then Early heard, "Finally seen . . . today . . . could be gone . . ." It was Mr. Pincer's voice, now sharp and ugly. "Up to us . . . all going, and I mean *all*." Early's heart felt as though it had sprouted wings and shot around the room. The words *finally seen*! And *today*!

Of course Mr. Pincer could have been talking about anything, but just *one* person, one earthshakingly important person, was gone. Dash! Dash, Dash, *Dash!* And maybe Mr. Pincer was threatening them all, saying Dash had to be found or they'd all be in trouble! Did this mean that Dash was *nearby*? And that he was *free*? And hadn't she maybe, just maybe, *seen* him this morning?

Early wanted to whoop, to shriek, but instead knelt down on the carpet, ready to hide behind the rubbery plant. Whoa! Mr. Pincer's door flew open, then closed again with a *bang*. Light, quick steps walked down the hallway. No one entered the room Early was crouching in.

She thought of Sum and Jubie down on the second floor, and realized she should get them all out of the building, and fast. They might be the first ones to be targeted if someone was after Dash. If criminals wanted to make him appear, all they had to do was capture and hold his family . . . *yikes*.

Standing, she crept to the open door. The buzz through the vent was now fainter. She peeked out into the hall, hoping her nose wasn't visible. Yes! Ms. Whissel was standing over her desk, with her back turned, head down, a phone held on one ear. Early whisked around the corner and tiptoed at top speed in the other direction, hoping for a stairwell.

An exit sign! Shoving open the heavy door, she hurried down one flight after another. When a door squeaked far above, she stopped. No steps. Was someone else listening? She froze, standing quietly until the door closed. Thudding down the last few stairs, she burst into the hallway by the Children's Library and ran inside.

Sum was reading aloud to Jubie, their heads bent low over a book. Early, out of breath, reached over to hug them both and stumbled onto Sum's lap.

"Oof!" Sum gasped.

"Get offa me!" Jubie giggled.

"Hurry, no time to lose!" Early huffed as she scrambled back up, but no one moved. "Now!" she finally shouted at them, grabbing their coats in her arms. "We gotta go!"

As the three scurried out the door, leaving behind a pile of books, the librarian looked after them. Mr. Tumble reached for the phone, hesitated, and began instead to straighten his desk. Seconds later, he walked over to the pile and moved it carefully onto a cart, lining up the spines. He straightened the pillows where Jubie had been playing and checked his watch.

Cover

"I think Dash is okay! Maybe *escaped*!" Early blurted, still breathing heavily as they hurried up the long flight of stairs to the train platform.

She'd refused to wear Sum's jacket, saying she was hot. "The meeting was about something that was gone but had to be found. I heard *slipping* and *ice*, and that could only be Dash, right? I only caught a few words, but I'm sure there was some kind of threat made to the library workers, plus Mr. Waive. Seemed like they *all* might be in trouble now." Early paused and bent over, a stitch in her side. She had an uncomfortable feeling that they were being followed. She looked back several times, but didn't see anything unusual.

"The three of us better not hang around here, waiting for them to catch up. They're looking for Dash, and who knows, he might be headed to the shelter this minute!"

Sum's face was trembly, transformed; so fragile yet filled with light that Early realized with a sinking fear that perhaps she'd spoken too soon. "I wasn't *sure* what they were saying. It's a *maybe*."

But Sum's face was brighter by the second. "If he's escaped, you know he'll find us. And when he does . . ."

Jubie's eyes were huge with fear. "The bad guys gonna *get* us?" he whispered. "I want Dash! Now!"

"No worries, son, I'm here," Sum said, her voice sounding calmer and stronger than it had in weeks. "But you've gotta do *exactly* what I say, when I say it, you understand? And don't give away any secrets!"

"Won't. Give away. Secrets." Jubie nodded.

"Good," Sum said. "Now, Early, baby, you tell me everything."

Early tried, sharing the research she'd done yesterday with Mr. Waive, and what she suspected. She was worried that Sum had added up these fragments and spun them into a solid truth, she sounded so strong. She didn't dare tell her about the profile in the alley. Well, it was too late now to hide the other things from her mother, and perhaps that was okay. Sum had just needed some fresh hope to keep going. Early shivered, and allowed Sum to wrap her in the jacket.

Dash, I'm sorry! she said to herself. *I got Sum all worked up now.*

Before she could listen for a reply, a new worry flooded her mind. "There's one thing we need to keep top secret, and that means you, too, Jubie."

Her brother nodded, his mouth open.

Early was now whispering, her mouth covered with one hand so that no one else on the train could hear. She hadn't been able to shake the scary feeling of being watched. "If the bad guys know we have this, it might be used to trap Dash again. That's the only possession we own that could possibly be important, although why, I don't know. No place to hide jewels inside it; we've turned every page, over and over. But Mr. Alslip was hinting something about a printing today, how it was like a footprint. . . ."

Sum was nodding. "The first print run can make a volume valuable," she whispered.

"That's *secret*," Jubie said in Early's ear.

"Yup. Where is it right now?" Early asked her mother.

"In a drawer," Sum said. "I slipped it in under our clothing."

"Zip the lip, Jubie," Sum warned.

He did, with one finger, then grinned and did it again.

The train couldn't move fast enough for the three Pearls.

Cover

Stepping in the front door, Sum huffed a sigh of relief. Early hurried ahead up the stairs, slipped a hand into the drawer in their cluster, touched the familiar cover, and grinned.

"Of course," Sum said, rubbing her arms. "What were we thinking? Got ourselves spooked! Now both of you wash hands before lunch." Sum was still luminous after the morning's news, Jubie, more bubbly than usual, and Early, quiet. The familiar noise and confusion of the shelter felt good to all three, and although the lunch line was particularly long that day, no one complained.

"Oh, here they are," Mrs. Happadee said half an hour later, her voice pretending to be cheerful. A police officer stood by her side. "Could I borrow you three for just a moment?" she asked politely. It was then that Early noticed a small crowd by the front door and more men in uniform.

The three Pearls hopped up, leaving lunch trays on the table.

"You got bad guys?" Jubie asked, his voice squeaky with excitement.

Both Sum and Early shushed him, but Mrs. Happadee simply reached for his hand as they all crossed the room.

A man with a ragged jacket, brown sock hat, and handcuffs looked down at the floor. When he turned his face, Early gasped.

It was Mr. Alslip! Something made her stay quiet, at least until she knew whether he'd done something good or bad.

Velma was in the crowd and stepped forward. "I saw him follow you three in the door. He was pretendin' to empty garbage, but I was watchin'. Sometimes I just know things. He saw you three head upstairs and still pretended to be busy, like he belonged, but followed you on up. When you three came down and he didn't, I thought I'd better take a look. Caught him red-handed, emptying your drawers into a big garbage bag. Grabbed him from behind."

Here Velma wheezed with delight. "Looked like a scared mouse, he did." She chortled. For the first time, Early felt a tiny bit sorry for the man.

"Oh, Velma!" Sum hugged her. "Thank you so much, all of you. But can I check that bag before you take him away? I'd feel better if I knew every last thing was in there. . . ."

Sum was taken to the office, where Mrs. Happadee had locked up the bag. Early and Jubie stood awkwardly to one side of the crowd, and Early glanced shyly at Al's face. He raised his head just enough to give her a quick wink.

She sent back the tiniest of nods, and at that moment she felt she'd captured his rhythm. Or maybe even changed it.

Sum was back in a moment. "Looks fine, Officer."

After the police and Al were gone, Mrs. Happadee walked the Pearls back to her office and said, "I have a room with a lock on the door for you three. Third floor, where some of the other families stay. You don't mind being on the floor that has a few dads, do you?"

"Oh, of course not. That's wonderful, Mrs. Happadee," Sum said. "You've been great!"

"No problem," she said, but looked puzzled. "Any reason that man might be after your things? No jewelry or anything. I mean, I didn't notice any when the policeman looked through it."

"I'm not sure," Sum said.

"It's a mystery," Early added quickly.

"No secrets." Jubie nodded. "Don't know any secrets."

Mrs. Happadee smiled at him. "Such lovely kids you have, Mrs. Pearl," she said as she took them up to their new room, Sum hugging the extra-large garbage bag that now held everything they owned.

Cover

"Oh, my," Mrs. Happadee said, and opened the window a crack. A metal safety guard prevented it from going any higher.

The room was one of those gloomy ones that shoe-rockin' Darren had been in. With the narrow window looking out on a wall, it was dark and smelled like a cross between wet coats on the train and used diapers.

The walls were peppered with sneaker prints, bad words written in pen, and jagged scratches, as if someone had been attacking the plaster with a knife. "I'll be right back with your sheets and blankets. And some cleaning supplies," Mrs. Happadee said.

Early went with her to help. As they gathered up bedding from the old cluster, Mrs. Happadee paused to look closely at a shiny piece of metal on the floor.

"Goodness, it's a razor blade!" she said. "Must have come in with that man. Awful!" She slipped it carefully into a front pocket on her shirt.

Sum, Early, and Jubie spent the afternoon scrubbing. The room needed a brighter light so they could read in bed, but it looked and smelled better. When the drawers had aired out, Sum carefully unloaded the black bag, folding each piece of clothing as if neatness would make the room feel more like home.

"Aw," she said, turning over *The First Book of Rhythms*. "This dear book is so beat up now." She frowned. "And it's got a new tear. How on earth did that happen?"

"Let's see." Early reached out a hand for it. A sharp, clean cut had been started at the end of the spine.

The cut was almost unnoticeable, maybe a third of an inch long, but too perfect to be a tear. "Whoa," Early breathed. "The razor blade. We need some tape."

Sum had turned away and was talking with Jubie. She didn't hear what Early had said, and Early didn't repeat it.

Frowning, she ran her finger down the rest of the spine, which was still in one piece, but lumpy. She turned the book sideways and tried to see inside the narrow, sturdy tunnel that was a part of the spine, but all was dark. Then she shook it and a crumb of dried glue fell out. Since both ends of the spine were open, Early had never thought that something could be hidden there. But what had Al been up to?

Sum had folded the empty black bag neatly inside a drawer. It was a heavy-duty garbage sack, just like the ones that families moving in and out of the shelter carried; the Pearls had never had one before. Al must have swiped it from a box near the front desk on his way in. Early pulled it out now. "Just checking to see if some part of the book fell inside," she said.

Sum, busy lining up toilet articles along the top of the dresser, nodded. Early crinkled open the bag and reached deep into every corner, running her finger along the seams.

She touched something tiny, tiny and hard — an object about the size of a dried pea, but not perfectly round.

Glad she was facing away from her mother and brother, Early opened her palm, holding it toward the window. It was then that the smallest of rainbows flashed against her skin, as if alive.

A diamond.

"Sum —" she whispered, then stopped, closed the hand, bent over, and coughed like mad. Her mind was racing. If Sum knew, she might have to tell the police, who might not believe that Dash was innocent in all this. She coughed some more, her fist against her mouth.

Her mother patted her on the back. "Must be all the dust," she murmured. "Go for a drink of water."

Early did, slipping the stone quickly into the pocket of her jeans. She walked with her hand flat on the leg of her pants, covering that tiniest of bumps in the fabric. The bathroom was full of kids and their moms, everyone talking and washing. Early shot into a stall and sat down. *Now what?* she wondered.

She couldn't stay in there all day, and her thoughts weren't getting any clearer. *Think, Early, think!* she said fiercely to herself as she stood, straightening her clothes. She then leaned over the row of sinks after drinking, water dripping from her mouth, and looked up at the mirror.

Dash said I was a rainbow. Diamonds hold rainbows. Maybe I can be as strong as a diamond, a pearl that's also a diamond! Dash would like that one. The thought even seemed a little familiar — *click!* — as if it were one of Dash's pictures.

But *hiding* this from Sum? It felt creepy; it was such a huge secret. Early shivered. And if she didn't tell, would she *really* be protecting the other three members of her family? Or just protecting some gang, bad people who might end up hurting the Pearls to get what they wanted?

Sometimes keeping a secret was the *worst* thing to do.

Cover

Much darker than the open sleeping area had been, their new room felt like a shoe box once the door was shut.

"Sum? Can you come sleep with me?" Jubie asked after a few minutes.

"Sure," Sum said, and Early thought she sounded relieved to climb down into Jubie's bunk.

Early flipped over for what felt like the hundredth time. The right-wrongs and good-bads were so confusing and hard to see!

She was *tired* of trying to understand and make choices. Tired, tired, *tired*.

"Okay, Early?" Sum whispered.

"Tired" was all she replied.

The only 100 percent untroubling thing she could think of that night was the plan for homes. Just moving that idea around in her head, looking at it from all sides, made her feel good. And tomorrow the tutoring room would be open again. Mr. John would be there.

Early drifted off, imagining how surprised and proud Dash would be. Moments later, there was a loud *bam-bam-bam!* from down the hall. "Police, open up!" shouted a voice. Early, Sum, and Jubie startled awake, and all had the same frightened memory: the pounding on their apartment door, the silence, the waiting, and the huge crash.

"Oh, no . . ." murmured Sum. Jubie began to whimper.

"Police!" the voice shouted again. They heard a door opening and a lot of unhappy shouting and crying. Someone thumped or fell against a wall.

"That isn't my stuff. It's not!"

The Pearls stayed behind their closed door, although Early got down in the lower bunk, with Sum and Jubie. Sum lay on the outside, facing the door. Jubie, in the middle, curled into a ball against his mother's back. "Don't! Don't let them come in," he moaned over and over.

Voices continued in the hallway long after the police had left, taking a woman with them. The Pearls heard Mrs. Happadee walking back and forth, quieting everyone down. Somewhere a child was sobbing. A bit later, there was the familiar bump-*drag* sound of black Hefty bags being pulled down the hallway, carting away a life.

We're getting used to the sound of emergencies, Early thought to herself. *I won't say it because that'll upset Jubie, but it's horrible and feels wrong.*

If we were in our own home, it would be quiet. Just the nighttime sounds of snow falling.

And not on a sad field, she added fiercely. *Not like the end of Langston's poem, "for when dreams go, / Life is a barren field frozen with snow."*

No barren field for us.

Early tried to imagine Dash's hand touching the side of her head. She thought about where he might be. The image of him back in that alley, wrapped in a blanket, was too miserable to fall asleep on.

So she pictured them all walking up to the yellow house they'd loved in Woodlawn, Sum and Dash holding hands, Early and Jubie running ahead up the front steps; everyone stamping the snow off outside their front door; Sum making them cocoa in a kitchen with blue walls.

Cover

Drugs was the word murmured in the breakfast line.

Isobel and Marcus's mom had been arrested last night. Early and Jubie looked at each other.

"What?" Early said. "I can't believe it! Poor Isobel and little Marcus — that's terrible!"

"Those guys all alone now? Who's taking care of them?" Jubie asked, his voice squeaky with worry.

"I'm sure the police took them somewhere safe," Sum said. "It's awful, but this kind of thing happens to kids all the time."

"Maybe they have some relatives," Early said. "I hope. Isobel's my new buddy, and we had plans together! She must be so scared."

"Yeah, if they took Sum away, it would be baaaaaaad, right, Early?" Jubie asked. "I hope Marcus got to bring his orange truck."

"I'm not going anywhere without you two — you can bet your booties," Sum said. "Settle down now and eat those eggs. Gotta keep up our strength."

Velma nodded slowly, straightening a pin with a rubber troll that was fastened to her coat. She smoothed the troll's hair, saying only, "We moms need to help each other. Because kids need their moms."

"Isn't that the truth," Sum said, and patted Velma's back. Everyone ate in silence for a few minutes; shelter meals were always more thoughtful after there'd been an emergency. It seemed like bad and hard things of one kind or another were always happening at Helping Hand.

When two police officers walked in the shelter doors just as everyone was clearing their plates and cups, Mrs. Happadee's shoulders sagged. "Not again," Early heard her say.

She took the police to her office. Sum, Early, and Jubie were heading up the stairs to their new room when Mrs. Happadee called after them.

"I've got some news you'll want to hear," she said to Sum. Sum froze, and her face looked so eager that Mrs. Happadee hurried to say, "Nothing settled, but this is more information than you've had so far."

"The kids and I stay together," Sum said. Turning to Jubie, she ordered, "I'm counting on you to sit quietly. Not a word now."

He nodded, making a zip-the-lip sign.

The three Pearls crowded into Mrs. Happadee's office with the police.

"Ma'am, turns out some of your suspicions were right. Your husband got pulled into some scary stuff. It's possible he had no idea what he was mixed up in."

A glance at Sum's face pulled the officer up short. He said, "We still have no idea where he is. I have to be honest about that. But we're getting a better picture of what went on. It could be that he was — or is, excuse me — just a person who got used as a game piece in someone else's crime."

Sum nodded, her shoulders sagging. "I'll take that as good news," she murmured, "although it's what I already thought. Please tell me everything. Everything you can."

The policeman shared a crazy story.

First, Mr. Alslip said he had wanted to be arrested. He identified himself as a Chicago Public Library employee and told the police he needed protection. He described the meeting that Early had tried to listen to, the one with Mr. Pincer, Ms. Whissel, and Mr. Waive. At least, he gave his version of it.

According to Mr. Alslip, Mr. Pincer had warned them all that they were in the midst of an international diamond-smuggling operation, part of which was being handled by a gang based in New York. He said they had to keep quiet.

Mr. Alslip then told the police about having kept the money Dash gave him for a book, out of fear. He described an address in Marquette Park where he said he'd delivered the cartons of books, then admitted he felt badly about what he'd done and didn't want any more harm to come to the Pearl family. He said he'd had no idea how bad things were until he bumped into Early at the library.

Early asked if the policeman remembered the address in Marquette Park. He looked surprised and shrugged. "Oh, it was an old warehouse with no numbers on it," he said. "Completely empty." Early frowned. Hadn't Mr. Alslip told her the building had a number?

Mr. Pincer and Ms. Whissel had both been arrested last night. And Mr. Pincer, it turned out, was a guy with a slippery past. An unemployed hatchet man for large industrial companies that needed to cut back, he had lied about a background in the library world, forged an appropriate resume, and been hired in recent months to help the Chicago Public Library balance its complicated budget. Ms. Whissel had appeared on his first day at Harold Washington, offering to work for free as a personal assistant. She explained that she was between jobs but had always wanted to experience library work. Mr. Pincer agreed, thinking he was getting a bargain. What he didn't realize was that this stranger was a part of a huge and clever crime ring that was following recent developments at the city libraries.

When a certain Mr. Scrub approached Mr. Pincer, offering a considerable amount of money to look the other way if this "bookseller" hired two of the Library Pages for a little extracurricular work, he was thrilled. A greedy man, he accepted immediately, having no idea that he was now in the hands of a circle of expert criminals, and that Mr. Scrub and Ms. Whissel had known each other for years.

Like Mr. Pincer, Mr. Alslip was a man careless with the lives of others, and when Mr. Scrub approached him, offering extra money to pick a working partner who was an innocent type, he didn't hesitate.

When Sum heard that, she dropped her head in her hands.

"A rat with regrets," Early murmured. "That's Mr. Alslip," she said, when the adults all looked at her.

Ms. Whissel had admitted to visiting the shelter in disguise, hoping to get a peek at the Pearls' possessions, but there had never been a moment when the open sleeping area had been empty enough for her to paw through them unseen. She had reported back to the others at the library. Early wondered just how selfless Al's trip had been. If Velma hadn't stopped him, would he have left with all they owned, including the mysterious diamond?

Early squirmed in her seat, laying her hand casually on top of the tiny stone still in her pants pocket. Did that make *her* a criminal, hiding this diamond?

Should she say she had it, right this minute? But what if that made Dash look not as innocent? What if it might seem like Dash had *known* there was a diamond in their apartment? And what would happen to them all if she *didn't* tell? The what-ifs swirled this way and that, making her dizzy.

A diamond . . . Early realized, right then, that there was power here, and that selling a stone like this could make many things possible.

It was a thought she didn't want to have. Suddenly, she understood how tempted Mr. Alslip must have been.

Cast, *from the Middle English* casten

Verb: to hurl, toss, or fling; to throw outward; to calculate or add numbers.

Noun: the throw of dice; a stroke of fortune or fate.

Cast

Two FBI agents arrived, and asked to talk to Sum alone. Mrs. Happadee shuffled Early and Jubie out before Sum could argue.

"What did I miss?" Early asked as soon as Sum came out. "What else?"

But Sum shook her head. "You heard most of it: They've caught some of the bad folks, and they now truly *believe* Dash is innocent. That's the greatest gift of all! But they're still missing pieces of the picture, details on the diamond-smuggling operation and who-all is involved. They kept asking me if Dash had ever mentioned the warehouse location. The one Mr. Alslip sent them to looked impossible. Completely abandoned. I couldn't help."

Interesting, Early thought. Clearly the rhythm of fear, a fluttering on-off beat, was preventing Mr. Alslip from telling them everything. Maybe he was still afraid of the gang members who hadn't yet been caught, the men he'd seen each time he dropped off the boxes.

"So the big, *big* news is that it's safe for our Dash to come out; he just has to somehow get told. One of the FBI agents told me that they wouldn't release anything about a famous stolen diamond being found or the suspected gem smuggling until they had more information, but they *would* show pictures of Dash, asking that he come forward for protection. They'd also say that his family was waiting." Here Sum's voice wobbled and she had to stop. No one had spelled out the worst possibility of all: that Dash was no longer alive.

Early was overjoyed, but also terrified. Did the police know as much as she did? Did they know there might be — no, *was* — another loose diamond involved, and close by? And that it might well be a stone from that most famous of *all* diamond heists? Was it *really* safe for Dash to appear?

"So we're all waiting," Sum was saying, as if everything had been solved. "Dash can truly *head home* now, and fill in the details for everyone. He feels so close, it's agony not to be able to reach out and grab him!"

Early nodded. She had to think, and wished at that moment that her brain were as hard and bright as a diamond, that stone with so many secrets. But a pearl, she reminded herself, comes from something uninvited and difficult, a grain of sand in an oyster, something that eventually, over time, becomes a thing of beauty. Better to be a pearl. "Can I lie down upstairs for a few minutes?"

"Of course, baby!"

Sum and Jubie took a load of laundry downstairs to do a wash while Early rested in the room, which was just what she wanted: a few minutes alone.

"Dash," she said urgently, and this time in a whisper. "*Dash!* I don't know what to do!"

She heard the grinding of a garbage truck somewhere outside.

She stared at the dark wall opposite their window and wished she could see a sliver of sky, or at least some color.

Maybe she should flush the diamond down the toilet and no one would ever know the Pearl family had been living with it.

Then she thought of all the people outside in the snow, people with cups, hopeful signs, and only a few quarters. She wished with all her heart that the diamond could fly magically out the shelter door and into some of those sad hands, answering dreams. Then she focused on one of the missing pieces that could be essential: the warehouse address.

Suddenly she heard Dash, loud and clear: *You can do this, not as hard as it seems.*

She sat straight up on the bed.

"Dash?" she whispered. And quite suddenly, she recognized something else. Everything here was connected, like the facets on that tiny stone in her pocket. Like the beat in Langston's book. On the last page, he'd written that "all men's lives, and every living thing" were related to rhythms of "time and space and wonder."

The *address*! An hourly beat of threes that in turn added to multiples of three . . . Why hadn't she seen this before? Mr. Alslip had practically told her!

The number was 369. It had to be.

But how could she let the police know? It would seem strange if Sum told them, after she'd just assured the FBI she didn't know anything. And would the police take a phone call from a kid, or even listen to her?

Early went through the adults who might be willing to help, jumped up, and grabbed a new pocket notebook. She carefully ripped out one page and began to write.

Cast

"I'm just gonna take a nice, hot shower, Sum. Is that okay?" Early asked as soon as Sum and Jubie came in the door.

"Sure, baby," Sum said.

Early stood, already hugging her towel, clean clothes, and shampoo bottle. Once out the door, she closed it and took off at a quick, silent run for the stairs.

Velma was on the first floor, slumped at one of the long tables where she often sat during the day.

"Velma!" Early called out. "Come on, we gotta talk!" She hurried Velma around the corner to the hallway in front of the tutoring room, which was locked and empty. It was hard to find a place in Helping Hand where you could be alone for a few moments.

Minutes later, Velma walked toward the shelter door, beaming. "Headed to glory. I'll tell them cops where to look, but just the bare bones. And I'll give 'em, you know, the goods. Ever'thing'll be perfect," she muttered, patting the huge pockets on her coat.

"Thanks, Velma, you're the best," Early said.

"Tell your mama I'm still watchin' her stuff," Velma called over her shoulder.

Cast

Velma did some inventing for Early. First she walked into the police station nearby and announced to one of the detectives that she was a friend of the Pearl family, over at Helping Hand, and that she had found a diamond on the floor in the shelter after the man with the black bag had been arrested. She handed it over.

Next she showed them the note printed carefully by Early, whose handwriting was tidier than hers. It said *369, warehouse in Marquette Park.* Velma claimed, in another little lie, that she'd overheard the man who was later arrested making a cell phone call and mentioning these words.

The police fed Velma a delicious pasta lunch after she'd shown them that she didn't have the teeth to bite into a sandwich. While they waited at the precinct for news, the FBI, accompanied by Chicago police detectives, sped back and forth through Marquette Park. And as they did, Velma told the officer waiting with her in the station the truth about the address: It had been given, in a kind of code, to Dashel Pearl by a colleague at the Chicago Public Library who had gotten him into the book business, a certain Mr. Alslip, and it was Dash's daughter, Early, who had just figured out her father's notes.

That afternoon, the case broke wide open: Bursting into a warehouse with the number 369 on the door, the officers found a group of nine armed men guarding neat piles of over a hundred books on a table, in an otherwise empty room. They were all wearing guns but had been watching TV with the sound on loud, and hadn't heard the FBI quietly removing the bars on a first-floor window and entering. All nine were arrested without anyone firing a shot. The men had clearly been living in the building; there was clothing, a garbage can filled with beer bottles, soda cans, and a soggy mass of fast-food containers. A quick search revealed the room where they'd held Dash, a nasty bathroom with one tiny window. They swore to the police that he had escaped.

That afternoon, after Velma had been driven back to the shelter by the police and the Pearls had heard the good but scary news, Sum went upstairs to lie down for a while before dinner, leaving Early and Jubie in the tutoring room.

Velma stopped in to talk with them. She placed a hand on Early's back. "You're a smart girl, and a life-changer. Gonna help your mama all she needs," Velma said.

"Hey, aren't I smart, too?" Jubie squeaked.

Velma patted his arm. "Of course you are. Just like your dad, I'll bet!"

Jubie flopped his head back and forth so vigorously that he dropped his blue truck, and had to scramble after it.

"My father loves Langston Hughes, and he sometimes says, 'What's the rhythm, Langston?' when he's trying to see things right," Early said.

"I like that," Velma said. "I'm gonna try askin' that same thing."

"It helps," Early said. "And thanks again, Velma. For everything."

"Early, you quite a girl," Velma said. "Jubie, keep drivin'. Come on now, it's time to go find your mama and tell her waitin' time is better than no time at all."

Click, *uncertain origin*

Noun: a brief, sharp sound sometimes traced to a mechanical device, as with a camera or computer; a part of some African languages.

Verb: to select; to become a success; to fit seamlessly together.

Click

Things were brighter, but also darker, in the days after they heard that Dash had been kidnapped but had apparently escaped.

The police told Sum that law enforcement officers at all levels were trying to find the connection between certain European crime rings and the messier New York group that had been working in Chicago. They warned the Pearls that it could be ages before they tracked down all of the criminals involved, but the men arrested at the Marquette Park warehouse stuck to the story that Dash had left there alive. The worry, of course, was that other members of the ring would find Dash, wanting to prevent him from saying anything before he realized he could safely go to the police.

One of the hardest things for the Pearls to hear was that no one knew what Dash had been told. Detectives and police were quite sure that he had been warned by his kidnappers not to show his face anywhere in Chicago. In other words, even if he escaped, he'd look guilty, which could hurt his family. He might have no idea that some of the criminals had been caught and the truth was out.

Oddly, the only picture the three Pearls still had of Dash was the one on his state identification card, as he hadn't either a license or passport, and all of their family pictures, the ones in their apartment, were gone. The face looking out was hardly familiar, it was so serious; Dash usually had a twinkle in his eye.

Copies of the picture went to every TV station and newspaper in Chicago, but there wasn't yet much of a story to be told. Sum wasn't sure what had been shown or when, but Mr. Waive was watching all the time and had seen Dash flash by on the evening news. There had been short articles in some of the Chicago papers.

Dash's old teacher was in the hospital by the time the arrests were made, and because he'd been forced into Mr. Pincer's office that day and threatened, he was able to add to the story the police heard from Mr. Alslip. Mr. Waive's testimony was invaluable. His memories helped detectives realize that Dash was no ordinary guy, but a man of integrity and rare promise.

Sadly, Mr. Waive was seriously ill. Living in the shelters had made him sicker; it seemed like colds and flus *loved* those places. Almost everyone got sick in there, but anyone with trouble breathing had an extra tough time. Early wrote a note to Mr. Waive and looked forward to seeing him again when he was released from the hospital.

Since the news about Dash, each day at Helping Hand felt endless. The three Pearls looked toward the front door again and again, hoping to see a glimpse of Dash's shoulder, his head, his jacket, his hand. For ages Sum worked on her job applications and letters down at the tables in sight of the entrance; all three watched and waited when the phone rang at the front desk and the guard wrote down a message. Early imagined Dash striding in the door one day during a mealtime, and the three of them shrieking and running over, knocking him down with the biggest hug anyone in the world had ever seen. Everyone in Helping Hand would cheer, like people do with famous sports players in a game. "Dash! Dash! Dash!" they'd be chanting, then "Rahhhhh!" as the joy swept on and on.

The only time Early felt the tiniest bit relaxed these days was when she was thinking about Home Dreams, which was what she'd decided to call her project. Without really knowing it, Early had started something amazing in the city of Chicago, an idea that grew like wildfire. Agencies working with homeless families had heard about this project through the director at Chicago HOPES, the tutoring organization working at Helping Hand, and everyone loved the idea. It allowed kids to speak, offered a solid solution to family heartbreak, and cost almost nothing to share.

In no time at all, Home Dreams were being mailed to the mayor of Chicago, some big foundations in the city, even the president of the United States. With thousands of kids in need of homes and ready for a dream, the letters just kept coming.

The return address on each was *Home Dreams*, followed by the name of one or another of the family shelters in the city. If you happened to open one of these packages, you'd find this cover letter, handwritten and copied on a Xerox machine:

Hi, my name is Early Pearl. Here's a picture of me – click! – with an armload of books. I'm eleven years old, and am staying in Helping Hand Shelter with my mom and brother. Something bad happened to my dad but I know he's trying to get back to us. When he does, that will be the best day ever.

Kids need grown-ups to help them get started in life, but they also need a home.

Imagine if you couldn't head home when you left your office tonight or if your kids couldn't head home after a day at school. No matter what age you are, you need a place to rest where you feel like you belong. A place to have friends and be with family, a place to feel safe and private, a place to make plans, a place to dream. A place to put down some roots, or as my dad used to say, "A place to go and grow."

Early went on to tell her story.

Soon other kids were telling their stories, too. Photographs were attached to each.

My name is Marcella. I'm nine. This is me — *click!* — in my favorite pink sweatshirt. My dad came here to work as a gardener, but broke his leg falling down some stairs one winter and couldn't go to a doctor. He tried to fix it himself by tying it to sticks, but it hurts all the time. It's hard for him to find good work now and he isn't as fast as he used to be. One leg is straight and one is crooked.

Here's the house I want to be in. If my family and me could live there, we would sing. My mom and dad and brother and I would plant so many vegetables in the yard that we would always have extras: pimientos, jalapeños, tomates, frijoles, cebollas, lechuga, calabazas. We would have vegetables for any neighbor who was hungry. We would freeze and pickle lots for the winter. My grandma would make her yummy pimiento jelly.

I would sleep on the second floor with my sisters, and we would have curtains that opened so that sun could come in and we could look out. We would make a shrine for the Virgin in front, under the tree, and anyone who wanted to say a prayer could stop in our yard and do that. Maybe we could put a seat there for people who are tired.

We would have our own stove and refrigerator and kitchen table. I would help with the cooking and dishes. We could love one another all the time in my family, and my mom would stop crying. My dad would feel better because maybe we could sell enough vegetables to fix his leg. My mom is a great cook and we could sell her tamales and burritos, too. Us kids could set up a table on the porch and make change for people who came to buy.

That is my dream.

My name is Johnny, and I am ten. This is me — click! — with a picture of my cat, Champ. He is a beauty. When the sheriff came to our apartment and made us go, we had to leave Champ behind. I put all the food I could find in his bowl, and, man, did I feel bad. It was tough. Maybe one day I'll go back to my neighborhood and he'll be waiting for me. Just washing his face with his paw, like nothing happened. Maybe other people have been feeding and brushing him while he waits. I sure hope so. I left his brush, his favorite old pillow, and his bowl on our front steps.

Here's the apartment I picked out, on the second floor of this empty building. I like it because it has a lot of big windows, and Champ could sit and look out. I could watch the street, too. I'd see my friends coming down the block on bikes. I'd see the school bus, and run downstairs at the last minute.

Maybe I'd share a bedroom with my big brother, and we could sleep late on the weekends. Our family could have our own kitchen again, and eat stuff whenever we got hungry, like even in the middle of the night.

My mom and dad could find better jobs because we could say we had a home. We'd find a sofa, and all sit together in our pajamas and watch TV at night, and no one would be yelling at anyone else.

We'd always be happy to have our own place to go, and never forget what it feels like to have no home. And if Champ is by the door waiting for me every day after school, that will be my special dream. I don't want nothing else.

Hi, my name is Belinda, but I call myself Aisha. I'm ten years old. Here I am — click! — with my magic hair band, the one with the blue sparkles.

Here's the home I want us to live in. It's made of brick, it's down on the ground, and so strong, it couldn't burn like our old apartment. Stone doesn't catch fire like wood, and I think brick is stone. My mom and us three kids lived with my grandma until the heater got flames, and then my grandma, my brother, and my baby sister died when we were running down the stairs and the walls fell on us. My mom was at work that night.

If my mom and me could live in this house, we could start a life. That's what my mom likes to think about. Starting a life. We both miss my grandma, Booker, and May Rose, but we try to think ahead. I don't talk too much about my grandma's hugs, or Booker and me playing hide-and-seek, or the baby giggling every time I tickled her. My mom says we got to keep going, and that working hard keeps you from going crazy.

If we got a chance to fix up this house, maybe we could have curtains with pink rosebuds and a couch. We could blow good-bye kisses to each other and no one would laugh at us. We could relax without strangers nearby. We could feel safe, in this stone house with no stairs.

My dream is that we sometimes get to forget the sad things. But I say a prayer every night for my grandma and Booker and little May, and I hope they know I love them. My mom says they will always be in our hearts. I think this means all of our souls could be together in this house.

Click

The cold continued to crush and encircle all within reach. And the snow! Early had never noticed so many kinds of snow.

In the past three weeks, she'd seen it blanket-heavy and round with shadows; fast and sharp, a horizontal sting laced with ice; slo-o-w, as deliberate and haunting as a poem.

Slow was when each flake landing on a sleeve or glove became a rhythm of circles: a tiny, symmetrical treasure. If you moved with care, a snow crystal on a sunny day had the sparkle of a gem caught and kept for an instant. *Diamonds for anyone,* Early thought to herself, *as free and plentiful as words!* She wondered why so much beauty, tumbling out of the sky or drifting from people's minds, goes unseen.

She knew the answer, even as she wondered: People get distracted by worries and sadness, and have to struggle to see anything else. They have to work hard to hold on to beauty, to hold fast to dreams and words; like Sum, who seemed to grow more fragile with each passing day. Early knew she had to hold fast for three and dream for them all, at least until Dash came home.

She had time to think about snow, secrets, and the hard choices people make in life. She wasn't back in school yet. The police hadn't arrested the top people in the smuggling ring, and Sum wasn't about to risk any more kidnapping; she needed her kids close at all times. She told Early that as soon as Dash "headed home," they'd move back to Woodlawn and Early could return to her old classroom.

Sometimes she wrote in the homemade notebooks but now that felt lonely. Early missed all of the friends she'd made. She hoped Darren, Aisha, Isobel, and Marcus were all doing okay, wherever they were. Maybe being together in a shelter was part of the reason they'd gotten to be close so fast. Life in a shelter was unpredictable and bumpy, that was for sure, and you could never count on someone being there for long. So if you liked a person or had something to say, *click!* There was no time to waste.

It was sad to think that she now couldn't find these kids because they had no addresses or home phones next to their names.

There were moments that week when it seemed to Early like everyone in the shelter hated one another. People couldn't be bothered to leave the bathroom clean for those who came after them. They didn't say sorry if they stepped on a heel or toe. They weren't thoughtful about radio noise or talking loudly, or they shouted at and slapped their kids. Sometimes life at Helping Hand felt like one huge story of misery. A rhythm of wrongs.

Early looked up the word *shelter* and added it to her notebook. Origin unknown: It had no root that anyone knew, which fit. It meant an enclosed area that offers protection against a threat, and sounded like its definition; the word started with a soft *shh* and ended with a tidy, hard sound, like a door closing. She liked that, as *shelter* now felt more like a place of safety than a place for the lost.

As each day went by with no Dash, Sum got quieter and quieter. Early began being the one to take Jubie down to breakfast each morning, as Sum "just wasn't up to it"; when she did get up, she always looked tired. She stopped fixing her hair nicely, and sometimes forgot even to comb it. She stopped applying for jobs.

She didn't seem to hear the kids, and she never felt like reading aloud. It was as if she'd had a burst of energy right when she heard the good news about Dash escaping, and then when he didn't show up at the shelter day after day after day, she kind of let go. Began to drift, and then to go under.

"I'm sorry, baby," she murmured to Jubie, when he tried to get her up, shaking her shoulder over and over. When Early reminded her that Dash would say they had to keep going, she only leaked tears. Just hearing the word *Dash* these days seemed to hurt.

Early got more and more frightened. One night at bedtime, after reading to Jubie, with Sum lying nearby, she turned out the light and then pleaded silently with her father: *Dash, where are you? Each day feels like forever and Sum's not okay! I'm doing my best, but we all miss you so much and I don't know what'll happen to us without you! Things are desperate and we need you, Dash! We need you, need you,* need *you!*

She waited in the dark, clearing a quiet place in her head for Dash to answer, trying not to cry herself.

There was only the crinkling of the hard plastic covers on their mattresses as Jubie and Sum tried to get comfortable, and the *tap-tap* of their window rattling, as winter roared through the narrow channel between the buildings.

Just as Early was falling asleep, she thought she felt Dash cup the side of her head with his hand. In an instant she was up on one elbow.

There was no one there. *Of course,* Early thought sadly. What did she expect? And right at that moment, clear as day, she heard Dash say, *Hold fast.*

Hold . . . fast. . . . Hold . . . fast. . . . She lay down again. The words beat a slow, whooshing rhythm that felt like the wings of birds in flight. Was that really Dash this time? Or . . . or was she imagining his voice now? Was this just the rhythm of her heart?

The thought was too scary and sad to allow, and she quickly covered it — *click!* — with memories of all the pictures that were once up on their wall in the Woodlawn apartment. The four of them on the steps of their building . . . Jubie under the table they ate on . . . Early reading . . . Sum blowing a kiss . . . Sunshine, laughing, running, scraped knees, macaroni stuck to an elbow, enough love and hope for a dozen families.

Click! Dash was behind the camera, finding four in three, over and over as if to erase forever a time when one might be gone.

Click! Click! Click!

Ice: the third week of February 2011

A bone-thin man with wild hair walked in the door of Helping Hand early one morning. He looked around, searching the faces nearby, and asked a question at the front desk.

A call was made and Mrs. Happadee came running. As she approached the young man, she threw out her arms as if to hug him, but then seeing his haunted expression, paused. She clasped his hand in both of hers, a long and warm greeting.

"Follow me," she murmured.

They started up the stairs, side by side yet silent, awash in what wasn't said. A police detective who had entered with the man followed behind, carrying a small metal briefcase. Noticing that it was difficult for the man to walk, the woman moved slowly. These two, who'd only just met, looked as though life had handed them a right-now miracle. *Joy* was too quiet a word.

At the top of the stairs, once a certain door was opened, four people held one another so fast that there was no room for anything but dreams. Shrieks were followed by sobs and a burble of "Dash! Dash! Dash!"

When the detective outside the door cleared his throat minutes later, Dash looked around, said, "Ahh," and picked up a slender book with a red paper cover. He ran one trembly finger down the spine.

"Hiding in plain sight," he marveled. "Undercover," he added, with a glimmer of his former grin. "*Research rhythms* was a good idea, all right."

Early blurted, "It was, it was! And I didn't see it, either, Dash. For ages."

Shooting his daughter a questioning look that was also a wanna-hear-more, Dash reached around the open door and handed the book to the man in uniform.

"Thank you, sir. We'll return it." The detective nodded and, popping it into the metal box, locked it with a key. After the police and Mrs. Happadee had left and the door to their room was closed, the four Pearls had the longest, saltiest, happiest, and gentlest hug any one of them had ever had. It was clear Dash's body hurt, and badly.

"First, I owe you three a huge apology," Dash said softly, "for wanting more than we had. For thinking there was an easy way to get it. For not recognizing the wrong that seemed right or the just-out-of-sight. For confusing and losing."

Dash hadn't caught up with the recent news until that morning. He'd happened to see his face in a newspaper crumpled in a train station garbage can, read the article, and hobbled over to the policeman on duty. Calls were made, a box for carrying possible valuables was picked up at the station, and the police drove him straight to Helping Hand and his family.

"Once I was kidnapped on that January day, knocked off my bike and thrown into a truck, it didn't take long to realize these folks thought I'd stolen something from them. They kept shouting, 'Ice! *Hot ice!*' at me, and when I still didn't understand, they shouted, 'Back-alley diamonds!'

"And then the light went on. *Back alley* meant stolen. They asked me what I'd done with *The First Book of Rhythms.* I was so upset with myself. How had I missed something so obvious? Every time I'd held that little book, I wondered why the spine was stiff and why it seemed to weigh more than it should."

"Ohhh," breathed Sum. *"Ohhh."*

"Yeah," Early murmured.

Dash, who was clearly in pain, stopped to cough and then catch his breath.

"My poor, dear, sweet baby," said Sum, rubbing his back. "Not your fault, any of this craziness."

Dash shook his head in between more coughing, as if to say, *But it was.*

Early jumped in. "I know, Dash. I couldn't believe it when the questions started to have answers. But I was scared to share because it might get you guys in trouble, even *more* trouble. Felt like I had to sit quiet." Her words poured out faster and faster, as if she'd upended a heavy bag of marbles. "I found a *second* diamond here in the shelter, after Mr. Alslip grabbed our stuff. Don't worry, the police have it already. I'll tell you guys the whole thing later."

"What!" Sum and Dash said, in one voice.

"Telling *seee*crets!" warned Jubie. "No telling about diamond stuff!"

"It's okay, son," Sum said. "The secrets are over."

Early, now on her feet, was waving her arms. "And then I figured out how that *first* diamond turned up on the floor in our apartment. I'd been sitting at the table with *The First Book of Rhythms* when those criminals came and knocked down the door. I think the book was crushed and one of the diamonds popped out the end of the spine. *Presto!* There it was, hidden in plain sight. And then that policeman, well, maybe he saw a rainbow under his shoe."

"You my girl, Early," Dash said softly, and with so much wonder that Early didn't think she'd ever heard sweeter words.

Swallowing, she rushed on. "Once I started believing what we'd had all along and *still* had, it got easier to see more undercover stuff. Like the three, six, nine address Mr. Alslip gave you in code, you know, the times in your notebook. The *rhythm* you saw on the day you disappeared. In case they wouldn't listen to a kid, I gave the building number to our friend Velma at the shelter here, and she took it to the precinct."

"Wow-ow!" Dash choked, and when he stopped coughing again, said, "And I only hoped someone had rescued that notebook, and — oh!"

Sum pulled it from inside her shirt and Dash rolled his eyes up in a blissful grin, as if to say *definitely rescued*, but then doubled over with another wave of coughing. She passed him Jubie's cough medicine.

"Early!" Sum said, her voice pretend angry. "You held all *that* in, baby?"

"Yup, and I'm soooo glad to let it out. I was just holding fast. No 'barren field,' you know?" She paused. "But I'm ready for zero secrets and no more lies."

"Yeah, we was shoe-rockin' spies!" Jubie crowed, and Early gave him a thumbs-up. "Before you told," he added, his lower lip shelving out.

"But we still are," Early laughed. "Spies don't *stop* spying, even when they aren't trying."

"Spies without lies." Dash nodded.

"And what about me, I'm reeeeal good at zip-the-lip!" Jubie crowed. "Zippity-lippity!"

Dash twinkled. "And you my man, Mr. Jubilation. Where would we all *be* without that zippy lip?"

Jubie echoed, "Yeah, your man!" and rolled back and forth happily on the floor.

After more cough syrup, Dash went on, his voice still strained, "Feel like I've gotta keep telling till it's all out. We're Dashsumearlyjubie, and like you said, no more secrets."

"Go on, baby," Sum said. "We'll be quiet."

Dash took a deep, shuddery breath and continued, "After I'd realized *Rhythms* was what they wanted, I was terrified for you three. I invented something quickly, trying to lure the kidnappers away from our apartment. I told them a sad thing had happened after I'd kept the book for my family: I'd taken it into work one day, in order to compare it to versions I could look at on the Internet. Then I fell asleep on the train on the way home, jumped up from my seat, and left the book behind.

"The criminals didn't know whether to believe me. They first tried using you three to scare me into talking, then tried starvation and, well, violent stuff."

"*Pow!* Gonna get those guys, *pee-ow! Pow-pow!*" Jubie muttered, shooting with his blue truck.

"Into jail," Dash added, "where they belong. I found out that gun games aren't great, son. Not when they're real. And not up close."

"Oh." Jubie's truck sank back to the floor.

"But melon and cherry fights in the summer, they're still good," Early suggested.

"Spitting seeds and pits, you got it." Dash grinned, a flash of his old self that faded as he returned to the story.

"When nothing worked, my kidnappers finally got to thinkin' that they should just clean house, if you get my meaning. After all, I clearly didn't know much until they'd explained about the ice, which was a very stupid thing for them to do, and I think some of them knew it as soon as it was out. And I'd learned, during all that questioning, that the old books Al and I had been handling were just a clever way to hide a fortune.

"You were so right, Early. The stones had all been stuffed into the spines of the smaller books, a very secure storage spot, because they could then be carried around or even change hands in the most public places. Those old cloth spines can be pretty indestructible, far stronger and more flexible than the modern ones. It was a weird form of laundering, making a dirty past less obvious, like criminals do with stolen money. This crime ring planned to move some famous diamonds safely through the hands of someone working at the Chicago Public Library — your silly Dash! — and from there they could be sold. Things would look good. Businesslike but innocent: a name from the CPL, an official book list. The volumes could then pass easily through security checks of many kinds. This was a much safer and more invisible travel plan than storing and carrying them in small bags or lockboxes.

"From what I overheard, I learned that once these stolen gemstones had been moved, thanks to the book spines, they could be altered in the tiniest way by any jeweler's diamond-cutting machine and would no longer be identifiable as the same stone. From the way the criminals were acting, I figured the diamonds stored in Langston's book were a particularly fine set of stones. That is, passing them along was the most dangerous part, and that's where Al and I came in. But then when I kept the book . . .

"The men were drinking one night downstairs, and I heard them fighting about who would 'take care of' me. I decided I'd rather fall out of a window than be shot by them and never found, so I did something pretty crazy: I stripped down to my underwear and rubbed my shoulders quickly with a cake of soap from the bathroom. Then I slid between the narrow window bars and out onto the roof. I can't believe I did it, but I think ice, *real* ice this time, helped. The bars had been wet earlier that day, as snow had melted in the sun. When the temperature dropped again, everything was coated in a clear, slippery film. First, one kind of dangerous ice almost got me killed, then another, just as slippery and treacherous, probably saved my life! Funny that *ice* can mean such different things, and that help and hurt can sometimes be so close.

"Once out the window, I was shaking so badly, I couldn't stand. Hearing voices and shouting, I knew I had no time to waste. I began to crawl, slipped on more ice, and rolled right onto a balcony below. When the men peered out of the open window minutes later, I was gone. From where I'd landed, I reached the fire escape, dropped down into an alley, and limped into the back door of a nearby restaurant. I begged them to hide me, which they did, in a kitchen bin with the dirty tablecloths. I'll tell you, spilled food never smelled so good. Who knows why the owner of that restaurant was so kind to *me*, a frightening-looking man in his underwear and socks, but if he hadn't been . . . well, we wouldn't be together today. No more Dashsumearlyjubie, that's for sure.

"The criminals, armed and drunk, combed the neighborhood for days. I was just plain lucky that this kind Lithuanian man, the owner of an old family restaurant, believed my story. He fed me and brought me warm clothes, dark sunglasses, a new sock hat, and a jacket with a huge hood. Next he drove me over to our old apartment, even though we both knew that might be dangerous. I saw what had happened. I might've died right there from shock and grief if the old lady down the hall hadn't heard my voice and opened her door a crack. She told me that you three had gone to a shelter, but she didn't know which one. I had hope.

"The restaurant owner later handed me train and bus fare cards, plus a list of all the city shelters so I could begin looking for my family. He tucked forty dollars in my pocket without me knowing, gave me his blessing, and told me to get back in touch once I'd found all of you. He was like a father to me, such a good man. I can't wait for you all to meet him.

"Since then I've been sleeping in Union Station at night and making my way from one shelter to another during the day, watching the doors to see if I could spot you three. I was afraid to go to the police, as the folks who'd kidnapped me said I'd be arrested for stealing the diamonds *and* they'd chase after my family once I was in jail. I didn't know whether to believe them, but didn't dare do anything else.

"And then, after I saw the news . . . well, here I am. And we four gotta head home as soon as we ever, ever can."

"You bet," Sum whispered.

"I could sometimes hear you talking to me," Early said. "In my head. Like there were rhythms in the air. And I might've seen you once when we whizzed by on the train, but then I thought I'd just wished you into being there."

"Yeah, we was *saaaaad*," Jubie trumpeted. "Sum got sad and mad when I got bad, but then I was *good*. And now I'm never lettin' go!" Jubie finished, hugging his father's foot, the only safely squeezable part of him, as hard as he could.

"Sad, mad, bad, then glad." Early grinned at Jubie, who gave her the Darren chin salute.

"Oh, yeah," Dash said softly. "Never lettin' go. I thought about you three so much that I believe I *was* here, in my head and my heart." He paused and touched Sum's cheek. "And the rhythms — I think Langston was doing his best to help us. I kept thinking of those lines from the poem 'Problems': 'But what would happen / If the last 4 was late?' And that kind of pushed me to keep going. Dang, was I ever *late*!"

"Dang." Jubie nodded.

"Hey, baby," Sum said tenderly. "Some good stuff. Major home-hunting work, especially on the part of your Early Pearl here. She came up with quite an idea, a project that is letting kids in shelters share their home dreams with rich and powerful folks who might be able to help."

"I was reading Langston's dream poems," Early said. "Think that's where it started."

"And I been workin' on clues," Jubie added. "And eatin' what they got."

"Wow," Dash said, his voice stronger. "Lucky thing I disappeared so you kids could get all that good growing done." And he winked at Sum. "If Early finds us our next home, and she just might, we'll call it Hold Fast. How's that? And Jubie, if you keep on with the spy work and veggies, you'll be big enough to catch bad guys in no time."

"Bad! Guys!" Jubie shouted happily.

"Oh, please," Sum said, rolling her eyes at Dash.

They spent the rest of the day soothing and resoothing, sorting rhythms, and filling one another in on every facet of this crazy, ice-laden time. They remembered the many people who had helped them return to four: Mr. Waive, Velma, the wonderful restaurant owner, their old neighbor in Woodlawn, Mrs. B. at the Hughes School, Mrs. Wormser at the library, Mrs. Happadee, and even Al. Last but not least there was Langston himself, whose words had helped them throughout.

They were told a bizarre detail that afternoon: This was actually the eighth anniversary, to the day, of the Antwerp Diamond Center heist. Strange symmetry was at work. A member of the FBI came to the shelter to return the Pearls' copy of *The First Book of Rhythms* and tell them that seven more diamonds had been carefully removed from the spine of the book.

"Seven!" Dash and Sum breathed in unison.

"Making nine," Early murmured. "Fits the rolling pattern."

"Rol-ling!" Jubie announced, vrooming his truck up and over the agent's large and shiny shoe.

The man went on to explain that should there be any rewards offered by original owners for the return of diamonds found in this Chicago raid, the Pearls would receive that money. Their family had, after all, helped in many ways with the recovery of a fortune. No guarantees, the agent cautioned, but it sure was a sparkly thought. He paused to admire Jubie's blue truck on his way out.

Meanwhile, Mrs. Happadee welcomed Dash to Helping Hand. She got him medical care right away; Dash's cracked ribs, dislocated knee, many torn tendons, and broken collarbone were bandaged. He was sent back to the shelter with vitamins and a supply of special protein bars to help him gain strength.

When the press heard the real story — a tale of dangerously twinkly ice of all kinds, a crash, a chase, and an innocent family that had slipped through the cracks — donations of clothing, toys, and books began pouring into Helping Hand. And, best of all, the Chicago Public Library assured Dash that a full-time job was waiting whenever he felt well enough to return. In the meantime, the Pearls were as cozy as could be in their tiny, dark oyster shell of a room.

The past few weeks had felt like years to this family. Ice seemed to have frozen time, and a beat of threes had hidden four, at least until today. Now, despite home time lost, it seemed likely that Dashsumearlyjubie would have another chance to hold fast.

Who could say what might happen when the world finished catching up with four Pearls, an old book of rhythms, many stolen diamonds, and a load of dreams?

NOTE

It is difficult to count the homeless.

Some hide, others aren't sure how to be seen, still others are too young to ask for help. On any given night in the United States, over one and a half million children find themselves without an address or a front door to call their own.

As of October 2011, the city of Chicago reported roughly fifteen thousand abandoned buildings, most the result of foreclosure. They sit silent, haunting the neighborhoods that surround them. With an estimated thirty thousand homeless kids in this city, the questions are obvious.

Luckily, so are the dreams.

ACKNOWLEDGMENTS

Many people and organizations helped me to write this book. I am deeply grateful to the estate of Langston Hughes for allowing me to reprint some of his work. Mr. Hughes, a world-famous poet, novelist, and speaker, was a man who started poor and without much steady support. Like the character Dashel Pearl, he held fast to his dreams.

In 1949, when Mr. Hughes was almost fifty years old, he accepted a job as a Visiting Lecturer on Poetry at the University of Chicago Laboratory Schools, a place known for their "learning by doing" approach. He stayed in Hyde Park, a South Side neighborhood right next to Woodlawn.

While at the Lab Schools, Mr. Hughes worked with kids from kindergarten all the way up to high school, and talked with teachers. Everyone young and old who spent time with him felt as though they'd been handed a gift, a way of experiencing the world that they could tuck in one pocket. Mr. Hughes was kind, liked to laugh, and yet was dead serious about his art. He believed that everyone, people of every sort of background and heritage, should be allowed to become what they wanted to become — with work and determination.

The First Book of Rhythms was published in 1954, and according to jacket notes, the book grew directly from the time he'd spent at Lab "introducing young people to the fascinations of rhythm."

I am also deeply grateful to my friends and colleagues Bob and Dorothy Strang, who both taught at the Laboratory Schools for many years. I borrowed a powerful line from one of Bob Strang's poems: "Words are free and plentiful," and it lives on in this book. Thank you, Bob. And if I hadn't been taking a walk with Dorothy one day many years ago, and if we hadn't seen a copy of *The First Book of Rhythms* in the window of a store . . . well, many things might not have happened.

The following Chicago organizations have all added tremendously to the making of this book: the Chicago Public Library, the Chicago Public Library Foundation, the Chicago Coalition for the Homeless, the Chicago Alliance to End Homelessness, Catholic Charities, Chicago HOPES, the Chicago Department of Family and Support Services, the Inspiration Cafe, and *StreetWise*, an impressive weekly publication sold by homeless or poverty-level vendors on the city streets. Thank you to the many individuals who took time to answer my questions and welcome me to several of Chicago's shelters. And thank you so much to those who shared their stories.

Thanks go to the following individuals for helping in many, many ways: Althea Klein, Barbara Engel, David Williams, Rick Kogan, Skip Hampton, Dick Barry, Kristin Ortman, Eileen Higgins, Becki Martello, Marguerite Brown, Rhona Frazin, Bernadette Nowakowski, Michael Nameche, Kelly Vanderstoep, Adam Conway, and Therese McGee.

The Harold Washington branch of the Chicago Public Library is a beautiful place, and the librarians at every level are helpful and friendly. I have altered a few of the internal physical details, but most of the setting is easily recognizable. The warehouse in Marquette Park is imaginary. Helping Hand Shelter is an invented name, but a real place — a beautifully run refuge for many families.

Last but not least, my family and dear friends, who put up with long periods of time in which I practically disappeared into this book. I can never thank my husband, Bill, and our three kids enough. My old friend Annie helped tremendously at a crossroads moment, offering encouragement of many kinds. Doe Coover, agent and friend, has read, reread, and cheered me on throughout. My editor, David Levithan, deserves heartfelt thanks for holding fast and holding on from the first moment we discussed this book, several years ago. Thanks times a thousand, David. And many thanks to Ellie Berger; Charisse Meloto; my patient production editor and copy editor, Rachael Hicks and Esther Lin; wonderful designer, Elizabeth Parisi; and everyone on the Scholastic team who has worked together to make this book a reality.

Michael McGuire, owner of a Hyde Park institution, Supreme Jewelers, took the time to teach me the ABCs of diamonds. For information on the 2003 Antwerp diamond robbery, I relied on Scott Andrew Selby and Greg Campbell's excellent 2010 book, *Flawless: Inside the Largest Diamond Heist in History.*

Brad Jonas, of Powell's Books, introduced me to some of the intricacies of the bookselling industry, and was generous, as always, in answering my many questions and offering research advice.

Any inaccuracies in portraying an institution or organization are entirely my fault. Facts on the homeless vary, depending on what you read and how statistics are collected and presented. Shelter rules also vary. Not to be questioned, however, are the harsh realities of homelessness. Sadly, they have nothing to do with fiction.